Fate's Call

*A Novella from
the world of the King's Riders*

Fate's Call

A Novella from the world

of

The King's Riders

by

C.A. Szarek

Fate's Call
C.A. Szarek

A Novella from the world of
The King's Riders

**Paper Dragon Publishing
North Richland Hills, TX**

eBook ISBN: 978-1-941151-14-3
Print ISBN: 978-1-941151-15-0

Published in the United States of America

Second eBook Edition: August, 2017
Third Print Edition: September, 2017

Other Books by C.A. Szarek

<u>The King's Riders — Epic Fantasy Romance</u>
Sword's Call (Book One)
Love's Call (Book Two)
Rogue's Call (Book Three)

<u>Crossing Forces — Romantic Suspense</u>
Collision Force (Book One)
Cole in Her Stocking (A Crossing Forces Christmas) — *FREE read!*
Chance Collision (Book Two)
Calculated Collision (Book Three)
Collision Control (Book Four)
Superior Collision (Book Five) — *Coming Soon!*

<u>Highland Secrets Trilogy — Historical Fantasy Romance</u>
The Tartan MP3 Player (Book One)
The Fae Ring (Book Two)
The Parchment Scroll (Book Three)

<u>Anthologies</u>
Deep in the Hearts of Texas — *FREE read!*
Story: Promise (A Crossing Forces Companion)

THE NORTH

Dragon's Tail
Mountains of Armour
Elfin River
Terraquist
Coire Isle
Greenwald
North Ascova
Bettian Valley
Tarvis
Hadrian's Place
Berat
Elfian Islands
South Ascova
Dalunas
Southern Strait
Penal Territory

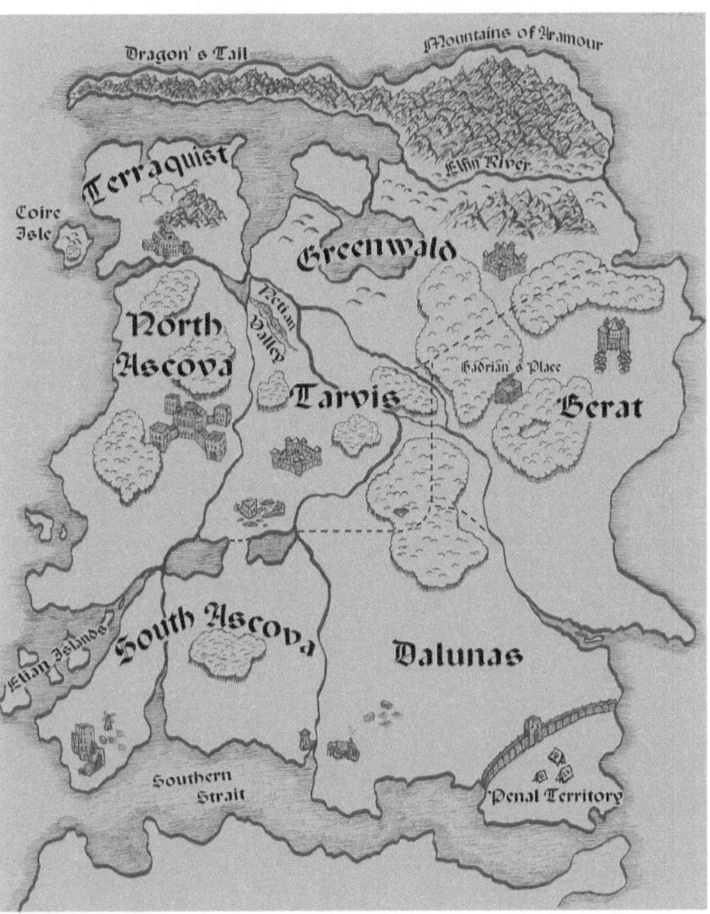

Dedication

To the ones who've been with me from the beginning! You know who you are!

A Note to the reader:

Like the two "alphabet" stories at the end of this book, Erron and Jarek were "born" to me in the form of a serial on my blog. This was before I was published (also mentioned at the end of this story, so make sure you check that out) and this is their story, but it's been edited and expanded to include new chapters and details that weren't there when it was in serial form.

I adored them when we "met" and I couldn't wait to revamp and share them with the world. So, if you've read the original version, please keep reading, the 2nd time around is so much better, expanded and edited!

If you're new to this story, I hope you adore it as much as I do!

Happy reading!

Chapter One

Erron ran.

Tears streamed down her face, blurring her vision, but still she forced one foot in front of the other. Moving forward.

I have to go. I have to get away.

Her chest heaved and her lungs burned, aching as she pushed air down and forced her muscles to work harder than they were used to.

Most likely, she wouldn't get away.

He'd probably punish her for fleeing but…she had to try.

She couldn't deal with her father anymore. Erron was done with his flippant moods, his heavy hand…and his rapes.

Since she'd turned eleven or so, and even before developing breasts or starting her monthly cycles, he had…taken what only a wife should be expected to give willingly to a husband.

Move. Go. Faster!

Sweat beaded her brow, dripped down her cheeks and even into her eyes, but she didn't pause. She had to go. She continued on as she made it into the market's center. It was busy and loud. Perhaps she could really disappear.

But…where can I go?

Erron glanced over her shoulder, then skittered around shops displaying their wares outside open doors in the warm spring morning. The sun was high in the cloudless clear blue sky, welcoming and bright.

It belied her urgency. Her terror.

Stalls and tables were crowded as people perused or bartered over desired items. A man cursed as she bolted around him, then another small group of three, making them jump apart.

She ignored them, keeping her legs in motion although they burned, calves throbbing as her muscles flexed.

Erron dashed down an alley and along an almost empty street. She was moving toward the outskirts of town now, nearing Lower Dalunas—not the best part of the Province. The prospect of brothels and less than reputable taverns didn't scare her more than her father.

What will he do when he catches me?

No. She couldn't think like that. She didn't regret taking this chance, and needed to make the situation the best she could.

Exhaustion was settling over her bones, begging her to stop, rest. Collapse. She panted puffs of air.

No. Keep. Going.

Her chest burned and her heart pounded, but she couldn't stop now.

She turned into another alley, risking another glimpse behind her. Was her father there? Did he know she'd run? Erron didn't slow, but the movement broke her rhythm and made her feet falter. She stumbled. Her line of vision wobbled and the edge of her shoe caught her skirt.

Down she went, throwing her hands out just in time to avoid landing on her face. Pain shot up her wrists as they absorbed the impact of her body, and her knees smarted because her dress wasn't padding enough on the hard ground.

"Oomph," whistled from her mouth. Her breath was gone now; she had to concentrate to get any air down. Her temples pounded with her rushing pulse, but she couldn't muster the strength to push herself off the ground, let alone to her feet. Her head swarmed with dizziness, but Erron refused to pass out.

"Are you all right?"

She startled and tremors skittered down her spine.

The voice was male, and she fought a full body shudder.

Where had he even come from? She'd not seen anyone when she'd entered the alley.

"Miss?"

Oh. Right.

He'd spoken and awaited an answer.

Erron tried to nod. Had her head even moved? Her thick plait fell forward. Escaped wisps tickled her cheek and forehead.

"Here, let me help you."

Brown boots entered her line of sight, then a hand. It was large and calloused, but something made her want to take it.

She lifted an aching wrist and placed shaking fingers against his.

Warm. His touch was warm and firm.

Strong.

Erron looked up as he pulled her to her feet without effort. Her eyes scanned his face and locked onto his. Deep brown. A dark gaze that made her stomach flip.

"Are you hurt?" he asked.

His brows drew together as he studied her; she couldn't find her voice. He was so handsome, with high cheekbones and clean-shaven cheeks. The man was concerned for her, too; it was all written over his expression.

Erron's heart stuttered. No one had ever looked at her like that before. Tears pricked her eyes.

He was tall and lean, sable locks shaggy and in need of a trim. He wore a dark leather apron over his tan long-sleeved linen tunic and brown breeches. Whatever his trade, he was a hard worker.

She yanked her hand from his grip and looked away. "I'm fine. Thank you," she whispered. She jumped as his fingertips brushed her jaw.

Her rescuer gripped her chin, guiding her face back to him.

I need to get away.

Erron didn't know this man; why was she letting him touch her? But when she met his deep brown eyes, she fell into their depths. She froze.

He wasn't hurting her. She wasn't afraid of him.

His touch sank into her skin, warmth spreading down her neck and into her shoulders. The gesture was casual and comforting…and wholly unfamiliar. It left her wanting more of his…gentleness.

"Why are you crying?" he whispered.

She blinked. Her tears were still flowing?

How did I not know?

"Are you injured?" he repeated.

"No."

His gaze raked her body, those brows still tight. Like he didn't believe her.

"Erron."

The barked demand of her name made her tremble.

Her heart plummeted to her toes.

No! He found me.

It'd been inevitable, right?

Her rescuer's hands fell from her face, and his eyes pulled away, settling over her shoulder on her father.

She didn't turn, but she sensed her biggest fear behind her. Erron clenched her jaw to fight the shudder. Had to steel her limbs. They weren't shaking from her hard run. Terror settled over her, chasing away the tender warmth of the stranger's touch. She wanted to bolt, but it wouldn't do her any good. She couldn't dare…again.

He was going to beat her. Or worse.

Erron swallowed and fought a wince.

The man in front of her noticed. He said nothing,

but his gaze went over her shoulder and then back to her face.

Could he sense her fear? Would he act on it?

She chided herself.

Don't be a fool. No one will save you.

"Jarek? What's taking you so long?"

Another male voiced sounded, making her jump.

Her eyes darted to the doorway to her left, several feet from where they were standing. Most likely, the back entry of a shop.

There was a large leather bag at her rescuer's feet she hadn't noticed before. He'd probably been sent to discard the refuse.

The man filling the frame was an older version of the one before her, his hair streaked with gray, but his face just as handsome as who had to be his son. He wiped his hands on a linen cloth as he leaned on the doorframe, irritation etched in his expression and his head cocked to one side.

"Coming, Da," her rescuer responded without looking away from her.

Erron's father, Norden, stepped to them.

He didn't hesitate to grab her upper arm, his fingers biting into her muscles until pain shot down to her elbow. He pulled her off-balance and she took a step back, which slammed her into his hard chest.

She winced.

"Erron, come along," he ordered, his tone gruff.

Alarm washed over her and she sucked in air. Needed to make her head stop spinning. She looked at the stranger and tried to focus on his eyes. "Thank you," she whispered.

Jarek. The man called him Jarek.

Jarek remained by her as she shivered in her father's grip, giving the barest nod of acknowledgment, before his gaze studied her father.

Her stomach roiled.

"Is everything all right?" the older man in the doorway asked, pushing off the building to come toward them.

Norden chuckled and she bit back a whimper. "Aye. My daughter and I were in the market, and I sent her to look for the blacksmith; do you know of one?" The lie fell from his lips, light as always, and very convincing.

Jarek's father relaxed, but he did not.

He continued to stare at her, then her father and back.

Erron shifted on her feet, her face hot; no doubt she was three shades of red. It was as though her rescuer could see through her. Part of her liked that; part of her was petrified Norden would perceive something that wasn't there. Something that would make her punishment worse.

"Yes, you're not far from the blacksmith. He's the next street over, but all the storefronts are on the opposite of the alleys. This is the back end," Jarek's father said.

"Thank you." Her father inclined his head. "Let's go, Erron. It's always like you to get lost." The slight admonition held the promise of violence.

She blinked away new tears and sniffled, fighting more quivers. Running had been the worst idea she'd ever had, and in the end, wouldn't be worth the price. Erron looked away from her rescuer, because she didn't want Jarek to notice any more than he already had. She couldn't look at her father's face, either.

"My son and I run the finest tanning shop in the Province if you're in need of anything. Jarek here makes the best deer hide boots around. Better than any cobbler." He slapped the younger man on the back.

Norden gave a very false smile. "We'll keep that in mind."

Jarek's gaze still burned into her.

"Please do. Good day." The older tanner inclined his head.

Erron's father did the same again.

She didn't miss the glare he sent Jarek's way. He must've noticed her rescuer was staring at her.

"Good day," she muttered in return.

Jarek's gaze never faltered, although he did return her gesture.

Norden yanked her down the alley, away from the young tanner.

Her stomach somersaulted. She'd never see him again.

That…felt…wrong.

Why?

Tightening his grip, her father's step quickened. As his stride was much longer than her own, he was dragging her and his fingers dug into her flesh even more.

She'd bruise, but that was nothing new. Black and blue marks on her arm were going to be the least of her worries.

When they got home.

Tears stung her eyes, but she refused to shed them anymore this day. Not for him.

Erron squared her shoulders and did her best to keep up.

----✂----

Jarek watched the stunning girl leave the alley with the man who'd called himself her father. Instinct screamed at him. Hit him in the gut as sure as a fist and spread all over his body, making him jumpy.

Something's wrong.

She'd been terrified. Shaking. That had only worsened when the bastard joined them. The grip on her arm hadn't looked violent, but he hadn't missed the girl's wince. So, the arse had hurt her, as well as scared her.

"Son?" his father, Kirgan, asked.

He shook himself but the worries didn't exit his mind.

Erron.

Her name was Erron, and she had to be the most beautiful girl he'd ever seen. She wasn't tall, would barely come up his shoulder, and was on the slender side—willowy, actually, as if she'd missed too many meals. Her pale blonde hair had been in a thick plait that landed at her tiny waist. Her dress had been as blue as her eyes, an older style with puffy sleeves and a higher neckline, but it hadn't hid the outline of her generous breasts.

Jarek never liked to see females upset, but looking into her petrified gaze had been different. The tears on her cheeks had just about killed him.

He didn't even know her.

Why had he touched her? The move had been…something he'd *had* to do. Hadn't even questioned the urge.

"Jarek?" His father put his hand on his arm and squeezed. "Is something wrong?"

He turned, meeting the dark eyes so like his own, and forced a smile. "Do you know that man?"

"No." Kirgan shook his head, his thick brows drawn together.

"Ever seen him at market?"

"Not that I can recall. What's wrong?"

"Something…something about what happened doesn't seem right, Da."

"Oh?"

His father was too trusting. Always had been. Jarek shook his head. "Never mind. I'm going to dump this." He gestured to the garbage that had brought him out back in the first place. "Go inside, I'll meet you shortly."

"All right. Don't toss that sack, it's got use left in it yet. Hurry, we've work to finish." Kirgan smiled.

He had trouble returning the gesture. "Aye. Of course."

Jarek handled his task quickly and headed back into their shop.

His thoughts were of nothing but Erron.

He had to find her. He needed to see her again.

Jarek didn't have much magic; he could light a fire with his mind and do a few spells here and there, mostly related to his tanning trade. He was no empath, but he'd always had good instincts. Never questioned his gut.

Something was off about Erron's father.

The man was dangerous.

He questioned the man's claim that they were looking for the blacksmith, even if Hem's shop was close. Jarek had trouble swallowing the idea that Erron had a tendency to get lost, as well. She hadn't looked worried over something simple; she'd been trembling. Terrified.

Why?

He needed to make sure she was all right.

Chapter Two

Jarek threw his tools down and shook his head. His concentration was gone. No amount of cursing was helping. He needed to focus, because he had an order for three sets of ladies' slippers to make for the new Duchess of Dalunas.

The ebony-haired beauty, Lady Aresha, had come in personally to put the request in. The designs were specific and complicated, including etchings, some embossing, and gold trim. Magic was going to be necessary, but it was nothing he couldn't handle.

If he did an exceptional job—and he would—she'd come back again. More coin for him and his father, and word of their business would spread to elite customers. Unfortunately, his mind consisted of one thing…one person.

Erron.

Why was she afraid of her father? The man should cherish her.

Did he beat her?

Every possible horrible scenario marched across his mind, tying his stomach in knots. Jarek shuddered. He needed a distraction.

No, he *needed* to work.

The ladies' slippers would be some of his finest

work, and he definitely wanted a chance to do more like them.

"Jarek, I'm going to market. The butcher wants to speak of trade."

He jolted at his father's voice and gritted back a curse.

Prayed Kirgan didn't notice he'd startled him. "Make sure he doesn't cheat you this time." Jarek offered his father a smile and rose from his seat. He stretched his arms and back, chuckling when the older man glared.

The look his father wore made him want to tease the master tanner more, but he held his tongue.

He followed Kirgan to the front door of their shop, giving him an affectionate pat on the shoulder. "Good luck, Da."

Irritation was gone from the older man's expression; he smiled, clasping Jarek's forearm. "Thank you, my boy."

"Kirgan! Jarek! Fine afternoon," the widow, Anais, called from across the street as she swept the front porch of her weaving shop.

A wide table Jarek had set up for her that morning sat out front, piled with baskets of various sizes. She had a rack of multicolored rugs hanging behind that, and a few other wares on display outside due to the warm weather.

He'd promised to help her take the heavy wood back inside her shop at the end of the business day.

They often traded services, and there was many a

night when she'd provided a hearty meal for the two bachelors.

Jarek was very fond of Anais; she was like a mother to him. He was amused at her obvious affinity for his da, too.

He smiled and waved, but his father looked away. He cocked an eyebrow and looked from one to the other.

Was his father *blushing*?

Jarek stared, fighting a gape.

Anais waved, smiling brightly and overtly trying to catch his father's eye. Her affection for his father was nothing new — and not a secret — usually ignored by the older man.

Did something happen to change that?

Kirgan muttered a greeting and shoved his hands into the pockets of his breeches. He looked down and shuffled off without another word.

The widow continued to sweep, whistling to herself. Apparently whatever had happened didn't bother her.

Jarek shook his head, laughing as he headed back to his work.

Anais was one of the sweetest people he knew, and had looked after him quite a bit since his mother had passed when he was twelve, some ten turns ago. If she could find happiness with his crotchety father, he had no qualms.

Kirgan, on the other hand, seemed as if he'd require some convincing.

Stubborn old man.

It made sense for them to be together. Her children were grown, as was Jarek. She had two daughters who were married and gone.

What was his father waiting for? It was a waste of time. Happiness had to be grasped with both hands.

Erron floated back into his mind. She wasn't happy.

Jarek would…love…to make her happy. His heart thundered.

Where had *that* come from?

He'd seen the girl *once*. In the back of his mind, a voice whispered that perhaps once was enough. He ignored it, staring at the work he was avoiding.

He couldn't remember ever seeing Erron or her father in Dalunas Main or even at market, and Kirgan rented a booth in the city square once a month to have more visibility to their customers. Jarek and his da took turns running it, and he often people-watched when he was there.

Could they be of another Province? Or from an outlying holding away from the city center?

Their clothes provided no clues. They hadn't been particularly rich, or obviously poor, other than being a touch out of the common styles he saw every day.

The rough man had asked about a blacksmith. That told Jarek nothing either, for the blacksmith forged more than weapons. Erron's father could be a farmer needing new tools before the spring planting.

He circled the room, his thoughts chaotic, his work

ignored, and he only had one slipper of the first pair complete. The design for it was right next to the piece of leather he'd been working, tacked to the table so he could easily study it.

Jarek really needed to work.

No.

He had to find her.

Rushing out of the shop, he called the widow's name.

"Lad? Is everything all right?" She headed to his side, broom still in her plump hand.

Anais looked pretty today, her dress bright purple hues that fit her personality. Her apron matched, but it was a lighter shade of lavender, and her fair hair was tied in a bun at her neck with a purple ribbon. She wore a pale kerchief on her head. Her cheeks were pink from exertion and her fair brows drawn tight.

He didn't like that he'd worried her. "It is, but I have to leave." He loosened his leather apron and tugged it off.

She took it from him without a word.

"Can you watch the shop?"

"Of course." Anais frowned and her blue eyes were concerned. "Are you certain nothing's wrong?"

Jarek flashed a smile and pressed a kiss into her cheek. "Everything will be fine. Just wait for my father…tell him I had to run an errand? I don't know when I'll be back."

At the mention of the master tanner, she beamed, nodding until her kerchief flapped. "I'll see you later, then. I'll start evening meal. The rabbit stew your da loves."

"That's my favorite as well, you know." He took a breath and made himself relax, then gave the older woman a quick hug she returned. "Thank you, Anais."

"Anytime, my lad."

He didn't answer. Just left at a jog, following the path his father had taken about an hour before. Jarek sent a quick prayer to the Blessed Spirit that he'd find Erron.

Limbs heavy, his chest constricted with crushing disappointment. He couldn't find her.

Jarek had scoured the market and the surrounding area—even three of the better taverns with rooms for rent. No sign of Erron or her father.

It was as if the whole exchange had been some phantom he'd imagined. Had his father not been a witness, he really would've thought he'd lost his mind.

Where the hell had they gone? Dalunas Main was not so large that one couldn't cover it in a day. Were they in Lower Dalunas?

He shuddered. *No.* For the girl's sake, it couldn't be.

Jarek wished he had tracking magic instead of skills that felt useless right now, associated with tanning and general household chores. How could it help find Erron?

Evening was settling, and with it, a chill in the air.

The breeze carried the scent of impending rain. Apprehension and disappointment skittered down his spine. He sent a quick prayer to the Blessed Spirit that she was warm, safe, and stayed dry for the night. Then admitted defeat. If he didn't head home, his father would worry. Not to mention Anais.

He jogged down the nearly empty streets. Didn't stop to chat with anyone he saw, but most were headed home for supper anyway, if not already there. It was past twilight, and the moon was on its way to dominate the sky after putting the sun to bed.

All the vendors in the square had been long packed up for the night, and most shops in the main business district had closed up, with darkened windows, except for candle and/or magic lighting coming from the residential sections of the building. Instead of looking abandoned, it was a reminder of home for him, since he and his father also lived where they worked.

Jarek passed inns and taverns, and even through closed doors, voices carried. People came and went there, doors opened and closed, but he didn't stop inside any, even the few he'd explored earlier while looking for her.

The scent of food floated thick in the air, making his stomach rumble, and he quickened his pace. He smelled spices and cooking meats; all kinds of foods. He hadn't taken time to eat midday meal; he'd been searching for Erron, so he had plans to devour as much of Anais' rabbit stew as his gut allowed.

A working girl called to him from an open window, but Jarek ignored her and kept going.

The neigh of horses made him smile when he went by the public stables. He couldn't see any, since they were all inside, but lights could be seen from around and under the main doors there, too.

Only two more streets and I'm home.

The first drop of rain hit his cheek right when he made it to the back entrance of the tanning shop. Jarek smiled and inhaled the clean, fresh scent.

Home.

The warm feeling of the familiar place was bittersweet, since he'd not found Erron. Was she safe at *her* home? Out of the rain and food in her belly?

He was still leery about her father. Worried for reasons he couldn't name. He sucked back a sigh and pushed the door open.

His father was laughing when Jarek entered their quarters, located on the opposite side of their storefront.

Laughing.

He stared for a moment, looking back and forth from Kirgan and the woman who sat at the table with him next to their main hearth.

The room was dim, but all the candles were lit, even the wall sconces. The hide decorations on the walls—made by his father when he'd been a journeyman tanner—were as home to Jarek as this place, but that wasn't what felt the most like *home* at the moment.

The scene before him was *right*.

Warmth from the fire embraced him, but also his affection for the older couple.

Why had he never noticed how lovely the widow was?

Anais wore no bonnet, nor the kerchief she'd sported during the day. Her fair hair was neatly coiffed at the back of her head, and her pretty face was radiant as she looked at his father.

Was he intruding? Somehow as hungry as he was, he wanted to leave them be.

"Jarek!" Kirgan exclaimed when he noticed him hovering in the doorway.

Anais shot to her feet as if she'd been caught doing something wrong, her full cheeks crimson.

He would've taken a moment to reassure her, but it would likely result in further embarrassment, and he didn't want that. Jarek loved the idea of them together.

"Where have you been, my boy? I was starting to worry," Kirgan remarked.

One corner of Jarek's mouth lifted. His father had looked content…and far too busy to be worried about his *adult* son. It warmed his heart anyway. At another time, he might've teased him, but internal amusement seemed better for now. He didn't want his da embarrassed, either.

"Let me get you something warm to eat," Anais rushed her words and fiddled with the wooden spoon in her hand.

Had she been feeding his father?

His smirk slid into a grin. "I'm fine," Jarek said, but it got him nowhere, and she hurried to the hearth.

As soon as she lifted the lid from the pot of stew she'd made, the pleasant aroma tickled his nose and his stomach growled full force. Double what it had earlier.

"All right, I'll eat."

Anais threw a smile over her shoulder as she ladled his supper into a bowl larger than he needed. "I thought as much; this is your favorite."

"You know us so well," his father mused.

Jarek glanced at him and saw tenderness as the older man gazed at the widow. He hadn't seen that before.

It's about damn time.

What had changed the awkwardness Kirgan had displayed this morning? Whatever it was, he was pleased. Shouldn't question it. He needed to encourage them without embarrassing either party.

His heart skipped as the stunning girl danced across his thoughts. Jarek didn't know Erron, yet he could imagine gazing at her in much the same way. She'd enchanted him.

"I should think so," Anais said, grinning as she came back to the table. "I've been caring for you both for turns."

His father nodded and Jarek slipped into his normal seat, his mind a jumble of Erron, his da, and the widow.

"Here you go, love." Anais put the bowl down in front of him.

The aroma tugged him back to the present—and his hunger. His stomach let out a snarl that made them all laugh.

"And you tried to say you weren't hungry, lad." She *tsked*.

He grinned. Wouldn't point out his hesitation had been because Jarek had crashed their little private supper. "Thank you," he said to them both, since his father handed him a spoon.

Anais slipped her arm around his shoulders and squeezed him in a hug before she sat back down next to his father. She'd moved too fast for him to return the affection, but he wanted to.

He took a bite of the thick bread she'd made instead, and groaned when the flavor of garlic butter hit his tongue. "So good."

She rewarded him with another grin. She'd told him many times that preparing food held no joy unless she could share it with others who would also delight in it. Delight, they always did. Anais was a fantastic cook.

The stew was next, and it was so delicious he had to remind himself to slow down; no one would take it from him. Jarek dipped his bread in the thick broth and took a bite, then spooned meat and tubers into his mouth.

"Where did you go?" his father asked.

They both watched him.

Too closely.

How much should he admit? They'd both likely

think him foolish. He didn't understand the drive to find the girl himself, so how could he explain it to his father and Anais?

"I looked for the lass," he admitted.

Kirgan's brows drew together. "But why?"

The widow's expression also held confusion, but Jarek didn't stop to recite the happening of that morning, although his father might've mentioned it.

"I can't explain it, Da. I need to find her."

His father looked even more troubled; his brow knitted tight and his mouth pulled down in a frown. He rested a calloused hand on Jarek's forearm. "Be sure you're not concerning yourself with something that *is* none of your concern."

He sighed. Didn't want to hear the sense in his father's caution. Jarek just needed to find her.

"He should find her, Kirgan, if he feels that strongly. Perhaps it's fate," Anais said softly.

So his father had told her what'd happened in the alley this morning. Jarek shot her a grateful look.

Kirgan looked deep in thought for a long moment before he spoke. "Fate?"

She smiled at them both. "Don't tell me such things are only for foolish women. I'm beyond believing that."

He grinned and his father chuckled.

"I'd never call you a fool, dearheart," Kirgan whispered.

Anais beamed and squeezed his hand.

"Smart man," Jarek put in. "If you did, Da, she

might never feed you again, and we all know what a horrible cook *I* am."

They all laughed.

His father and the widow shared a glance that melted into a stare, as if he wasn't there.

Jarek shifted on his seat. Odd to be uncomfortable in his own home.

Big sky blue eyes and a flaxen plait entered his mind again.

Why was Erron haunting him? Did it really mean something?

Was there such a thing as fate, as Anais had said?

He excused himself from the table.

His father and Anais barely noticed.

Jarek was fine with that. When she retired for the evening — provided it was to her own bed — he'd tell his father that they had his blessing.

Perhaps it'd assist Kirgan along with things, although based on what'd happened at supper, maybe his father had finally girded himself against shyness.

He laughed and shook his head. What a thought *that* was.

Jarek busied himself preparing for bed, but the fair-haired girl wouldn't exit his mind. He was more determined than ever to find Erron.

Chapter Three

er arms shook, aching from wrist to shoulder as she pushed the plow. Erron's back throbbed, muscles straining as she did the job minus Angus, their plow horse. *Punishment* for running off the other day on their way to market in Dalunas Main. However, physical labor was preferable to lying beneath him naked while he took what only a husband should.

She shuddered. He'd done *that* last night.

Screaming and fighting him didn't help. If she pounded his chest and kicked, he would hit her back. Her father was bigger, stronger, and hurt her when he put his hands on her, not to mention when he shoved inside her.

Erron had long learned he was quicker to finish and leave her be if she didn't respond to him in any way. Perhaps now anger would keep him away from her longer than normal. She prayed for a fortnight or two.

Her father had ranted and raved that she'd run. He'd demanded to know why—what he'd done to deserve her attempted abandonment. That was laughable, but she hadn't. He would've beaten her.

She hadn't answered his demands, either. She'd

sat by the hearth while he'd paced and yelled, with her head hung low and her hands in her lap.

As it was, he hadn't hit her for running. He'd ordered her to bathe then to his bed. After he'd finished with her, he'd ordered her to a sevenday of plowing with no horse.

She was near the end of her punishment period. Only today remained, until sunset, and her body was bruised all over. Agony owned her limbs, but at least the pain was from labor and not her father's belt.

Erron assumed she'd signed her own decree of doom. The small holding they managed would be her prison. There was no way Norden would take her back to Dalunas Main. As he'd hollered, she'd broken his trust.

She would never see the tanner again.

The dark eyed stare of her rescuer floated into her mind.

Jarek.

His name was Jarek. If she closed her eyes she could see every detail of his concerned expression. His handsome face, his gentle touch…

If only for a moment, he'd *cared* about her.

Was he married?

It would be pleasant to be with a man like him. So different from…what she knew.

Who was she trying to fool?

Even if the tanner was unwed, it was unlikely he'd ever want *her*.

Damaged. Impure.

No one would have her if the truth got out. Her father had ruined any chances of a good marriage for her.

Several of the surrounding family farm holdings had sons. Any one of them would make a fine husband. She'd been of marriageable age for several turns. Although, she was recently one and twenty, and none had offered for her, so what did it matter?

Erron chided herself for girlish fantasies.

Her mother had passed away almost ten turns before. Her father had gone mad with grief. One moment, he'd clutched her tightly because she resembled her mother, and the next, he pushed her way claiming the same reason.

Not long after, he'd demanded she fill her mother's place in his bed. Barely eleven, he'd taken her innocence, despite kicking and screaming. Her father had crushed her, body and spirit.

Erron wouldn't let him defeat her completely. But, as the turns went on, her endurance waivered with every beating, every rape. Something inside her wouldn't let her give up, even though a part of her was resigned to her fate. She'd learned to survive.

She'd begged, pleaded, and sent countless prayers to the Blessed Spirit, but had been forsaken. She was trapped with her father.

Norden would kill her or make her bear his children.

Every time he forced himself into her, fear and pain froze her heart that he'd leave her with his bastard.

If it happened, everyone would know what went on behind the closed doors of their home.

Whore.

She bit her lip to hold back threatening tears. A pregnancy had never occurred, though she'd bled monthly since age three and ten.

Perhaps that was the Blessed Spirit's one concession.

"Erron."

Her name was a gruff command and she bit back a gulp, squaring her shoulders before meeting his pale blue gaze. "Yes, Father?"

"You've almost finished." Norden gestured to the smallest of their three fields.

Erron was covered in sweat, agony settling over her whole body, but she wouldn't complain. "Yes, Father." She swallowed as she stared at his unreadable expression.

"Use the horse for the rest."

"Yes, Father."

"I expect my supper at the normal time, and you're taking too long."

She lowered her head, eyes blurring with tears. Never would she give him the satisfaction of seeing her cry. Besides, it would likely save her from his heavy hand.

He said nothing as he turned to go and neither did she.

Erron waited until his footsteps were no longer audible before she went to the barn to get Angus. At least the old horse was a friend.

----✂----

She stared at the bowl in front of her, no real appetite for its contents.

Her father ate with vigor, as was normal for him, having demanded she refill his plate twice before she'd even had a chance to sit down. His grunts of appreciation were the only compliments she ever received. Norden ate her food without complaint. That, at least, was preferable to a slap across the face.

Erron's limbs weighed as much as the plow, every muscle aching and throbbing. If she didn't soak in the bathtub, she wouldn't be able to move in the morning.

The farm had to be worked, so that wasn't an option. Hopefully she could sneak into the barn for a bath without notice. She'd wait until her father fell asleep.

"We're going to market in the morning." Her father's words were muffled, his mouth full of stew.

Her head reared up and their gazes collided.

Norden cocked his head to one side.

Erron's heart pounded. She should've masked her surprise. Shouldn't have moved so fast. He'd likely hit her —

"What's wrong with you?" he snapped.

"N-n-nothing, Father."

He stared a moment longer, her heart thundered so hard her vision blurred.

She bit back the urge to suck in air, and fought for

a serene expression. Erron wanted to look away, but she didn't dare. There was nothing he liked more than slapping her when she was caught unaware.

"I have business with the blacksmith."

"I am to accompany you?" She prayed her tone was even. She let her gaze dart around their modest cottage. The fire in the largest hearth was the only thing that felt welcoming, despite the familiar surroundings.

This place had lost its feeling of home for her the day her mother died.

It was her prison.

The other hearth was on the opposite side of the structure, and it was smaller. Supposed to be hers, to warm her tiny sleeping quarters, but Norden didn't always allow her to light it. Like now, it was dark and cold, so her room would be as well.

Erron would cope with that, as long as he didn't order her to his bed. She could get warm in the barn during her bath, and perhaps steal an unused horse blanket and sneak it into her room.

"Of course," her father growled. "I do not trust you here alone."

"Yes, Father." Her heart threatened to burst from her chest. After running from him, she never imagined he'd take her back into Dalunas Main at all, let alone so soon.

Jarek.

She could see Jarek again.

"Erron?"

"Yes, Father?"

"If you run from me again, I will kill you."

Erron's stomach roiled, and what little supper she'd forced down threatened to rise and spill. She fought the bile because he was staring, awaiting her acknowledgment.

Only when she nodded did Norden release her from his gaze, but fear skittered across her shoulders and down her spine.

His words were matter-of-fact and even, as if he'd commented on the coming rain or the harvest. But no less true. He *would* kill her and not pause to regret it for even a second.

She locked onto the picture of Jarek in her mind. Could she see her tanner again?

The possibility of missing the opportunity scared her even more than her father's vow.

Chapter Four

The closer they got to Dalunas Main, the harder her heart cantered. She gripped the reins of her mare, Fancy, until her knuckles whitened.

She'd see Jarek again.

Erron spared a glance at her father and squared her shoulders.

He *couldn't* know her plans.

How would she go about it, anyway?

Norden never left her alone. The memory of his promise last night at dinner darted into her mind. Made her shiver. Her father *would* kill her if she ran.

If he caught her. Nay — *when* he caught her.

It wasn't fair to drag Jarek into her mess of a life. He had a father, too. What if he had a mother, siblings? They'd all be in jeopardy.

Once again, the possibility of the tanner being married danced into her thoughts. What *if* he had a wife?

Erron's heart stuttered.

No.

It was possible. He was grown, of a marrying age, probably a turn or two older than her twenty-one, if not a few more than that.

Tears burned her eyes and she swallowed against

the lump in her throat.

What was wrong with her?

The constriction in her chest made no sense. She'd seen the tanner *once*. Why did the thought of him being married bother her so much? It wasn't like he would volunteer to save her, anyway.

"Erron," her father snapped.

She jolted in her saddle and met his irritated gaze.

"Pay attention. Take control of Fancy. If she stumbles because of you, I will take it out on your hide."

Erron nodded, but her father had already looked away.

He ranted about how he was *allowing* her to ride *his* horse. He grumbled that he should've made her walk.

She sighed. It was no use daydreaming about the handsome tanner. She'd never get away from her father.

When they got into Dalunas Main, Erron's hopes lifted. Her father directed them to an inn. They were staying in town overnight. Although they often made day-trips to market, Norden never brought them into the city center and not returned back home the same day, no matter the hour.

After complaining about the costs of stabling their horses and for the suitable room, her father paid the rotund innkeeper. The older man had introduced himself as Felton, and led them up rickety stairs to their room. He asked Erron if she required anything.

"She'll fetch our supper later," her father snapped.

She winced, because Felton nodded and gazed at her with sympathetic brown eyes. He excused himself with a slight bow.

Erron looked around the small room, her heart tripping over itself. If Norden wanted to overpower her, there was no place for her to retreat to. The bed took up much of the room, with a window to the left that opened over the busy streets.

The furniture was sparse, only a chest of drawers and a cloudy mirror. The privy was in the corner. Small, but private. At least the room smelled and looked clean.

Glancing back at the bed, her stomach clenched. *One bed.* She'd have to share it with her father.

"I'm going out."

She met her father's eyes as he spoke.

"Do not move from this room," he barked.

He was leaving…*without* her?

Erron stared. Tried not to gape. She jolted, but couldn't react even at his hard order. Needed to maintain her calm farce, while her stomach flipped and her pulse made her temples throb. "Yes, sir." She forced words out and a nod for good measure.

With a grunt, Norden turned on his heel and left, shutting the door with a resounding *thud.*

She studied the warped wood, frozen.

He left me alone?

Norden had *never* left her alone.

Blessed Spirit, he'd actually left her *alone!*

Erron rushed to the window. Looking down, she

scanned the crowds of people moving toward the busy market center. There were people on foot, people on horseback or leading pack animals. There was a row of carts lumbering on its way, led by large beasts of burden.

It was early, so the rushing crowd included the vendors that needed to set up for the day.

She spotted her father's retreating figure easily enough. He was headed down the road that led to the blacksmith's shop.

Just two streets over from there was her tanner.

Jarek.

How could she get to him?

---✂︎---

Jarek sighed.

Anais continued her conversation with the butcher's wife, even though she'd concluded her meat shopping.

Why he'd agreed to her request to go with her to market was beyond him. He was a human packhorse. The woman had bought one of *everything.*

His arms ached with her four—*four full*—baskets hanging at every angle. It was enough food to feed an army.

Her smile had been bright and her face full of adoration for his father, so Jarek couldn't refuse her. She was oblivious to his annoyance as well, but he had no intention to offend her.

"Ready, Jarek, love?" Anais asked several

moments later.

"Of course. Where to next?"

Home, please!

"I think I've gotten everything we need."

Thank the Blessed Spirit.

He flashed a smile. "I thought you would *never* say so."

"Oh, hush. You're a strapping young lad, you can handle it." She patted his chest and caressed his cheek.

Jarek's smile slid into a sheepish grin. "My arms won't be right for days."

Anais mock-glared at him. "You're not too old to have your hide tanned."

He laughed out loud, shaking his head. "I'm two and twenty! What's too old?"

"Hmmm, you'll always be my lad."

His heart warmed. Had he not had arms full of groceries, he would've hugged her. "Thank you, Anais."

She nodded, her mouth curved in a soft smile. "Home, then?"

"Before my arms fall off would be preferable."

Anais swatted at his rear end as they headed out of the butcher shop and Jarek chuckled.

They fell into step and easy conversation as they headed down the road. He genuinely enjoyed her company. How could he nudge his father into making her an official — permanent — part of their family? The sooner the better.

He led her down the shortest path to their homes;

Anais followed him across the street and he gestured for her to step ahead of him as the path narrowed for several feet before widening again. Out of the corner of his eye, he caught a familiar figure.

Jarek stilled, then whirled.

The widow paused, her expression curious as she met his eyes.

He looked away from her, his gaze locked onto Erron's father as he headed into the blacksmith's shop.

"Jarek? Is something wrong?"

Erron.

"I…need to go." His heart thundered. Where was she? He scanned the street. Among the people that were coming and going, he didn't spot her anywhere.

Was she in Dalunas Main? Was she all right?

"What are you talking about?" Anais asked, her tone concerned and her pretty face marred by a frown.

Jarek forced himself to meet her crystal blue eyes. "Remember the girl from the alley last sevenday, who Da and I told you about?"

"Yes…"

"Her father just went into Hem's shop."

"Go, lad." No hesitation in her voice whatsoever.

He nodded curtly. Anais' support made his decision. "Will you be all right with all these things?"

"Aye, love. Go."

Jarek dropped a kiss on her forehead and she smiled.

She patted his cheek again, before taking the four baskets as he whispered his thanks, with a promise to help her with whatever she needed later.

He slipped away then. He had to find Erron.

Jarek headed toward the blacksmith's shop.

Erron's father glanced over his shoulder just inside the open area under the master blacksmith's, awning.

It was all he could do to not duck out of sight. Instinct told Jarek that Erron's father could *not* spot him.

Where's that coming from?

He got close enough to hear their conversation, hidden from view behind the large cart displaying farming tools Hem had outside and to the right of the storefront.

The older man was a good friend to his father, and would no doubt have interesting questions if Jarek was caught hiding.

People passed by, going about their day with little notice, so he didn't move from his chosen spot.

Whatever business they had contained some hefty bargaining, but Hem wasn't letting the fair-haired man off lightly.

Jarek admired him for that.

A noisy cart lumbered down the street, the driver shouting at his lead horse and cutting him off from the conversation in the shop. He cursed, but he had no choice but to wait for them to pass.

"….longer?" was the only word he caught from Erron's father as *clop-clop* from the horses' hooves faded.

"Perhaps an hour," Hem answered.

"I shall wait."

"As you wish."

Jarek's heart skipped. Erron's father would be in the shop for a while. He could see her for an hour.

Where is she?

He heard the clang of hammer against anvil from Hem or one of his men working, and strained to hear the men's continued conversation. He needed to find out where Erron was. Jarek inched closer.

"*The Rusty Nail* has better whores," Hem said.

Jarek peered over the cart in time to see the nearly toothless grin the master blacksmith sported.

"I've my daughter with me. That's why I chose Felton's place. Cleaner, anyway."

"Aye, s'pose so."

Jarek's mind raced in rhythm with his heartbeat. *'Felton's place'* was a tavern and inn called *Old Spirits*, at the center of town.

If he ran, he could make it in ten minutes.

He stared at the busy street. It wasn't yet noon. Many people were still meandering in and out of the various surrounding shops or following the road into market.

Jarek jogged into the crowd. People would just have to get out of his way.

The alleyways might be faster, but he didn't want to have to devise a path, or have to avoid people dumping dirty water on his head, or worse, trash.

The most direct route would be better, even if he'd have to dart in and out of traffic like a thief running from the marshals.

There wasn't much time.

Erron.

He was going to her.

Chapter Five

Erron sighed as she stared out the window. She'd pulled the lone chair in the room up to it to watch the activities below. She'd not brought needlepoint, which she hated anyway, or any of her many mending projects, so there was little else for her to do.

It was a warm sunny day. The kind of day that fed her desire to be out in it, doing—anything.

The room behind her held little appeal, even though she could've benefited from a nap. Afternoon sleeping was not something she was familiar with, and a part of her feared her father's return, so she didn't dare test the clean white linens or see if the mattress was as soft as it looked.

The furs were thicker than anything she had at home, so they'd be warm, but Erron dreaded crawling under them. Tonight she'd have to share that space with her father, so no matter how cozy and comfortable the bed was, she already dreaded it.

She was a tad hungry but she was better off waiting for Norden's return before calling for something to eat. She didn't want to chance angering him when he'd given her a small reprieve—leaving her alone in the inn. If she cost him coin for an extra meal, he wouldn't like it. Erron didn't dare venture down to the tavern either way.

Jarek danced in and out of her thoughts.

How could she get to him?

She'd been a fool to think it was even possible, even though she knew where his tanning shop was. Besides, she was stuck following her father's *order*.

People came and went, shouted, laughed, compared purchases and bargained with crafters selling their wares. Children played, only to be admonished to move out of the road.

A dark head moving through the crowds with some speed caught her eye.

Her heart thundered.

Jarek.

How she could tell at that distance was a mystery, but it *was* him. There was no doubt.

He was coming toward her.

Toward the *Old Spirits Inn and Tavern.* But...*how* had he known where she was? How had he known she was even in Dalunas Main?

Erron rushed to her feet at the moment he looked up.

Their gazes collided and he froze under her window.

"I'm coming up." Jarek's voice was thick.

She nodded, her body flushing with warmth. *Anticipation.* Heat warred with trepidation, tearing at her. She...wanted him to come to her, but...her father could return at any moment.

No matter how innocent, even a conversation would fuel Norden's wrath.

Her legs took her to the door. Her hand reached, opened it.

Jarek's booted feet were loud as they pounded up the stairwell.

Then she was enveloped. His scent, a mixture of spiced soap, leather, and the spring day outside tickled her nose. Her cheek touched his chest as he tugged her closer. His tunic was rough linen, made for the work he did, but it didn't bother her.

She heard the door close, but was only aware of *him*. His arms around her, pulling her ever closer. Erron got lost in the feel of him, the scent of him. She wanted to burrow closer.

Warm. Safe.

Jarek set her away from him, his dark eyes wide as they met hers. "I'm...sorry. I don't know why I did that." His hands cupped her shoulders, but then he let his arms fall away.

It left her cold.

Her mind scrambled for words. The embrace was over much too soon. It left her...*wanting.*

What was wrong with her?

This is crazy. And dangerous. "I..."

"Actually...I'm not sorry. I had to...touch you," he plowed on, as if she'd not made an attempt to speak. "I can't explain why."

Embarrassment crept up Erron's neck, scorched her face on the way to her ears. She stared. "How...?"

He took a step forward.

She didn't move away.

His cheeks were flushed with color across his high cheekbones and straight nose from his run, his too-long dark hair windblown, and the heat of his body still warmed her, even though they were no longer touching.

Jarek gripped her chin and studied her until she burned all over.

She averted her eyes.

"Erron."

Her name on his tongue brought her gaze back, made her whole form burn even hotter. It sounded...*perfect*. The fact that he'd remembered her name wasn't a surprise.

Why?

"Jarek," she whispered.

He didn't look any more shocked that she'd recalled his either.

His eyes slipped closed, but only for a moment. Then he refocused on her, like she was the only thing in the world that mattered. "I had to see you."

Reality was fading away, but Erron had to grasp it. This wasn't safe. "How did you even find me?" She needed to move away from him. He had to stop touching her. She couldn't think.

She just stared up into his dark eyes.

Would he try to kiss her?

Stop. What are you even thinking? That would be a disaster.

"I was at market. I saw your…father." The way he said the last word made her cringe.

Jarek couldn't know, could he?

"Did you speak to him?"

"No." He shook his head. His hair flopped over his forehead and she wanted to reach up to shove it back, away from his gorgeous eyes.

Her breath exited on a whoosh. At least Norden didn't get the chance to harm him.

"I needed to see you. I haven't stopped thinking about you since that day," Jarek said.

"I…I…I've thought about you, too." The admission made her heart pound.

He wore a smile that made her stomach flip. Jarek guided her to the bed, and they sat as if it was the most natural thing in the world.

Erron reached for his hand and he entwined their fingers, as if they'd touched as such dozens of times.

They talked for what seemed hours.

Jarek kept glancing out the window. "He'll be back soon."

"I'll only be in town until tomorrow," she murmured, her chest tightening. Breathing hurt and her heart sped up. She had to swallow and blink back tears. Erron didn't want him to notice her emotion, because he'd likely comment on it.

He squeezed her hand. "What is… this… connection?"

"I don't know."

"You feel it." It wasn't a question.

She nodded.

"I don't want to leave you," he whispered.

"I…don't…want you to go. But…" Erron shook her head. She wanted to reach out, wrap herself around him.

What's happening to me?

There was a *connection*, like Jarek had said. One that scared and excited her. It broke her heart, too, because she wouldn't be able to do anything about it.

Her father owned her, and she could never have freedom.

Never have her tanner.

Erron sucked back a whimper and fought the urge to double over and hug her middle.

"I know. He's probably already on his way back." Jarek's voice was thick, but it tugged her back to him.

He was still here, sitting next to her.

How could she say goodbye?

His handsome face was drawn, but he wore a small smile. He caressed her cheek. "We'll see each other again," he whispered.

No we won't.

She nodded, a lump closing off her throat. She'd never be that lucky. Erron averted her gaze, but couldn't bear not seeing his eyes and had to look back at him. "Go. Please," she croaked. Her hand lingered in his, but for only a moment longer.

He pressed a kiss into her knuckles, and his smile lost a touch of its sadness. Determination settled in those brown orbs, and he pulled her to her feet, into another embrace.

Erron wrapped her arms around him and crushed her eyes shut, plastering her face to his chest. He was so much taller than her, but the size of his body didn't scare her, it made her feel protected. She sank into the heat around her, praying he'd never let her go.

Too soon, Jarek released her and she rubbed her arm, missing the warmth of his touch. She watched him retreat and agony spread from her heart down her limbs, cooling her body until she shivered. Loss was a living, writhing thing around her, and she didn't stop to question it.

None of this makes sense.

With one hand on the doorknob, Jarek looked over his shoulder. "Erron." His eyes bored into hers. "I *will* come for you."

Then he was gone, so he didn't hear her whisper, "I believe you." Tremors shot down her spine as her mind and body warred.

Was his vow good or bad?

- - -✄- - -

Jarek didn't want to leave her. He stared up at the open window — her window — and waited a moment.

She didn't come over to look down upon him.

His chest constricted. Leaving her felt…*wrong*. He wanted to take her with him.

Whoa…that's crazy.

How could he *feel* so much for a girl he'd seen literally two times?

He shook his head and forced himself away from the place, or he'd run back up that stairwell, break down the door, and steal her away.

Would she protest?

Erron had said she'd been thinking of him, too.

Jarek's heart tripped. He…wanted her. Not just physically. "I *have* gone crazy," he whispered.

He'd hurried to get to her, but his step was slow on his retreat. Every lift of his boots was an effort, his instincts screaming he was going the wrong way.

He needed to stay with Erron. He wanted to hold her, kiss her. Why the hell hadn't he kissed her goodbye?

She probably wouldn't have let him, anyway. Hugging her twice hadn't been enough. She'd finally wrapped her arms around him the second time.

Erron had been crying, too. It wrenched his heart for reasons he couldn't name. Why had she been so sad?

Jarek couldn't let her go, and he wanted to make sure she never cried again.

She'd told him where she lived. He hadn't decided what to do with that information, had he? He'd promised to go to her. Could he?

He kept an eye out for her father, but didn't see or pass him as he made his way home.

Damn, he could've had more time with her.

By the time he reached the tanning shop's storefront, his heart was in his stomach, his shoulders slumped. Never in his life was the sense he'd made a mistake so strong.

Jarek should have stayed with Erron.

His father's voice caught his attention, and he looked up from his musings. What he saw made him trip into the doorjamb. His caught himself on the wall just inside the shop.

Anais was in his father's arms.

The older couple was beaming at each other.

The smile faded from Kirgan's face, replaced with concern. "Son, are you all right?"

Anais slipped from his father's arms and rushed to him. "My lad?"

Jarek met her eyes and managed a smile. "I'm fine, Anais, really." He dropped a kiss on her cheek. "You two just surprised me, is all."

His father chuckled and pulled the widow back to his side, slipping his arm around her waist, as if he couldn't bear not touching her.

He knew the feeling well.

Erron.

"We've some news," Kirgan said.

"Oh?" he asked.

The widow's cheeks were crimson and Jarek couldn't hold back his grin.

His father looked at her, a tender smile on his face, holding her even tighter to his side. The older man finally looked back at him. "We're to be wed."

"Well, it's about damn time!" Jarek exclaimed, sweeping his new mother into a hug.

Over her shoulder, his father struggled to hold

onto a mock-glare but lost the battle. His grin took turns off his face.

Jarek winked.

Happiness for them warred with envy.

He pulled away from Anais and she returned to his father, slipping her arm around his waist and kissing his weathered cheek.

Jarek stared, unable to look away from the obviously love as they gazed at each other.

"Lad, is something wrong?" Anais' voice mirrored the worry that had again settled in his father's expression.

Jarek took a breath. "No. Nothing's wrong."

They exchanged a glance shouting neither believed him.

"Listen, I have some news, too."

Kirgan arched a bushy dark brow bidding him to continue.

"Let's sit." Jarek gestured to the largest workbench in the shop. As he talked, he formulated his plan.

Chapter Six

Erron forced herself to remain seated on the bed as Jarek's footsteps faded down the stairs. He *had* to go. Her vision blurred and she wiped the tears away. The last thing she needed was her father to notice she'd been crying and demand to know why. Norden would twist it, make it her fault, and beat her.

She didn't trust herself to go to the window and watch her tanner walking away. She wouldn't be able to keep from calling out to him, begging him not to leave.

Or worse—go after him. Run away with him.

What the hell are you thinking?

Her father *would* kill her.

Why had she told Jarek where they lived?

I will come for you.

His words bounced around in her head. Erron believed him. No matter, what good would it do? Could he want her?

Her heart pounded.

When Jarek found out the truth, he wouldn't anymore. No one would.

As much as that hurt, she couldn't blame him. She was damaged, impure. A shudder wracked her body and tears cascaded.

She'd always been stuck with her father; that wasn't new. But now she knew what it was to crave something else. And feel just as hopeless about getting it.

"Erron, get yourself together," she whispered, swiping her hands down her cheeks, then rubbing her eyes. Her father could be back any moment.

Norden returned within minutes, and called down for food, beating her to it. He wasn't talkative and he didn't even inquire how her morning had been.

That night they shared the bed, but he didn't touch her.

Erron couldn't sleep. Fear that her father would wake and reach for her kept her alert, wary. At home, when he finished, he always let her flee to her own room after barking, "I'm done with you."

She hated the phrase, it always made her wince, but she hated sharing a bed with him more. Every time Jarek's handsome face popped into her mind, shame washed over her and she scooted a little closer to the edge of the bed.

Erron trembled and clutched the furs up to her neck. Tears fell silently, but thankfully didn't disturb Norden, who slept on his side, his back to her, snoring softly.

She called herself a fool for grieving her situation. She'd had turns to do so and had very much considered herself over it.

Resigned to her fate.

Why did Jarek have to come along and make her

want more?

She sealed her eyes shut and prayed for sleep.

----✄----

The ride home was coated in misery, but it was pretty close to how she was feeling, so maybe for once the Blessed Spirit was on her side. The rain poured down on them, but it helped disguise the tears that wouldn't stop.

Jarek consumed Erron's thoughts. She'd only seen him once. It wasn't nearly enough, even though she had no business craving more.

Waste of time anyway.

Two nights, one day in Dalunas Main and she'd not left the *Old Spirits Inn and Tavern* at all. Even the privy was inside the small room she'd shared with her father.

At least he'd not touched her. Being around people had given her a reprieve other than being alone. Evidently, Norden didn't want the outside world to know what went on behind the closed doors of their home.

He'd come and gone several times, barking harsh threats each time he'd left her. Despite that, her stomach fluttered as soon as he was gone. Erron waited for her tanner, but he didn't come to her. She even called to him mentally, as if she possessed the magic necessary to get a response.

She'd told him she was leaving the morning after she'd seen him, because she hadn't known otherwise, of course, but she missed him more every moment he'd failed to show up.

She clung to the white mare as they trudged in the mud and rain. Fancy's mane was plastered to her long neck, but Erron weaved her fingers into the coarse hair anyway, holding onto the reins with the other. She needed to feel something, even the soaked warm hide of her mount beneath her fingertips.

"Erron, sit up and hold onto that horse properly," her father barked.

Wincing, she did as ordered, slipping a little further into her cloak so he couldn't see her face.

When they got home, she helped Norden tend the horses. He was gruff with her like always, but he didn't touch her.

In the house, he watched while she heated the water for a bath without comment. Her heart sped up with every moment he stayed by the hearth. Erron's hands shook as she filled the tub by the warm fire, managing bucket after bucket of steaming water by herself. She didn't want his assistance. She wanted him to retreat to his room.

She had no desire to bathe naked in front of him, or worse — *with* him.

"Hurry with your washing so the water will not chill for my bath," her father said.

"Yes, Father." She breathed a sigh of relief as he disappeared into his quarters.

Erron didn't question why he'd let her bathe first, but she did appreciate it. She wanted to soak in the tub;

her muscles were sore from the ride, but she couldn't take the risk. She'd have to reserve that for a private bath in the barn tomorrow or the next day.

She washed as fast as she could, donning a floor length, long sleeved, high-necked chemise with too-damp skin. She shoved her arms into it, heart in her throat. Her stomach fluttered and her heart took off when Erron heard the creak of her father's door, but he hadn't reappeared just yet.

The need to crawl into her own bed and bar the door was all consuming. There was no lock on the small room she slept in. If Norden wanted her in his bed, he usually ordered her there after evening meal.

"Father, your bath is ready," she called. No way was she going into his room. Her hands trembled as she put out a folded bathing sheet for him.

He said nothing as he came back to the fireplace, but he started to unbutton his shirt. His breeches were already beltless and hanging open.

Erron averted her eyes from his wide chest, covered with springy fair hair, and breathed a sigh of relief when he said nothing. She didn't want to stay in the main room of the cottage and give him reason for ordering her to his bed, but she couldn't run away, either.

She sucked in air and commanded her heart to calm, then waited until she heard the splash of water. She slipped into her room, muttering a "Goodnight," he ignored.

Tears slid down her cheeks as she lay in bed. She

tugged the thin blankets up and shivered from the chill in the air. Norden hadn't allowed her to light a fire in her tiny hearth. She'd be cold, like she was most nights. Erron hadn't been able to grab a horse blanket, because her father had been by her side when they'd cared for the horses after the trip.

She turned on her side, tucking the fur under the front of her body and the back. Erron drew her knees up, curling into a ball and rocking. Hoping to build warmth.

Even though she'd hated every moment of sleeping next to Norden at the *Old Spirits Inn and Tavern*, at least the bed had been comfortable and the furs warm.

She crushed her eyes shut and tried to fight the flowing tears.

Erron had been foolish to think anyone could change her reality.

Jarek's handsome smiling face danced into her mind and she gritted her teeth. He was a dream she couldn't have.

She could only pray the Blessed Spirit would keep her from her father's bed this night.

Chapter Seven

She looked up when someone called her name. Her heart stuttered and she had to order her feet to stop so she wouldn't fall on her face. Erron blinked but the vision didn't clear.

He's real…

Jarek, astride a dark horse, was on the road at the edge of the field she was plowing with Angus. He was so handsome, so familiar he stole her breath and her head swam.

She pulled the old gray horse to a halt and he whinnied, but she ignored him, her eyes on the man who hadn't left her thoughts in the sevenday she'd been home from Dalunas Main.

Erron glanced over her shoulder at the cottage she shared with her father. All was quiet, but would he come barging out at any moment?

She shuddered and looked back at her tanner. She struggled to remember what Norden had been doing — or where he'd been — when she'd left to begin her daily farming duties.

The smile on Jarek's face made her body flush. She shoved the wisps of hair from her eyes and swiped at her sweaty cheeks. She must look awful.

"Erron," the tanner repeated, hopping down from

his mount.

Was he real?

He laughed. "Aye, I'm real. I'm really here."

Heat crept into her cheeks. She'd spoken aloud?

Jarek jumped the fence and landed beside her.

Angus didn't like the sudden movement and shifted his hooves, nickering as he tossed his head back.

She couldn't reassure the old plow horse. Erron could only stare at her tanner. She looked up into his dark eyes. Didn't pull away when he gripped her hand and caressed the back of it with his thumb. The move was soothing and warmed her. It left her wanting again.

She shouldn't…couldn't.

"I told you I'd come for you. Did you not believe me?"

"I don't know what to say," she confessed.

Jarek flashed a smile and dipped down. He tugged her into his arms, and his mouth came down on hers.

Erron had dreamed about this—her first real kiss. Reality was so much better.

With the first move of his lips over hers, she snaked her arms around his neck and he pulled her closer. The warmth of his body consumed her and she inched even closer, opening her mouth under his.

Jarek pushed his tongue inside, touching hers. She tentatively did the same. Their tongues rubbed, entwined. Dueled.

Someone moaned.

Heat suffused her body, traveling down her arms,

spine and settling in her belly, low. Erron held onto him tighter, having no choice but to meld against him, because her shaking legs threatened to fail her.

He tightened his arms around her, holding her up, and kissed her harder.

The hard ridge of his arousal pressed into her belly, but she wasn't afraid, she was…excited. She wanted more. Her stomach flipped and the warmth spread even lower, making her achy.

Jarek broke the kiss.

Her vision danced, and she gripped his forearms to stay on her feet.

He groaned as his gaze raked her face. "You have no idea how long I've wanted to do that," he breathed.

Renewed heat rushed her face, and Erron looked away. Her eyes swept the field and she froze in his arms. Anyone could've seen them.

"What's wrong?" Concern clouded his expression.

She pulled away from him gently and Jarek released her. Erron was cold without his arms around her. She shivered.

"Erron…"

"My father could've seen us."

His brow furrowed. "About that—"

"You wouldn't understand. You need to leave before he sees you." Her words were rushed and she had to bite her bottom lip to keep it from trembling. Tears burned and she swallowed a sob. She would not cry in front of him.

Jarek crossed his arms over his chest, his brows

tight, and a frown marring his handsome face. "I'm not going anywhere."

Erron stared.

What can I say?

She couldn't tell him the truth...

As much as it would probably hurry his departure, she couldn't bear the shame of him knowing, or seeing disgust in those beautiful brown orbs.

"I wish to speak with your father, so let him see us."

She shook her head and took a step back. The wooden plow handle hit her hip and she wobbled.

Jarek's hand shot out and steadied her.

Her heart thundered in her ears, her blood rushing from her face in a wave. She needed to thank him for keeping her from falling, but the words wouldn't form.

What can he have to say to Father?

"Tell me what's wrong."

"I...can't," Erron whispered.

"Why?"

"It...it...doesn't matter. Just go. Before he sees you."

---✁---

Jarek stared. Erron was practically pushing him to his horse.

What the hell?

She wanted him to leave?

The way she'd returned his kiss couldn't have been faked. She wanted him as much as he wanted her.

She'd been right there with him…until he'd told her he wanted to talk to her father.

Erron hadn't even asked him what he wanted to discuss. Her skin had paled out so much he'd feared she'd pass out.

She wavered on her feet and in his grip. She'd even pushed his hand off after he'd kept her from tripping backwards over the plow.

He'd always known something was wrong. A daughter didn't fear her father — and it was fear written all over Erron — like that without reason.

But what's the reason?

Cupping her shoulders, he shook her gently. "Erron, stop."

Her sky blue eyes went so wide the whites were visible all around. "Jarek…" Her voice broke, her body trembled beneath his hands, and she threw a glance over her shoulder, worrying her bottom lip.

"I'm not going anywhere." He drew her back into his arms, expecting her to fight him. Jarek wouldn't be deterred.

Her shoulders slumped and she collapsed against his chest.

He smoothed the pale hair that had escaped her thick plait. Blessed Spirit, he wanted to see the flaxen waves loose. Run his fingers through them.

Jarek wanted Erron.

It felt so good to hold her, he'd take what he could get for now.

"Why did you come?" she asked, the sound

muffled against the fabric of his beige tunic.

"For you, of course."

She pulled back and met his gaze. "Whatever for?"

Jarek's heart skipped a beat. He didn't like the break of their physical contact, so he settled his hands on her shoulders, like he'd done before.

What would she say to his confession?

They didn't know each other. They'd met literally two times before today, yet he was drawn to her with no explanation.

Was it some latent magic? Something he couldn't grasp? Maybe Erron had magic, too? Stronger than his.

He couldn't see into the future, but this stunning girl was a part of his own as sure as a vision confirming it. There was no doubt.

She didn't love him. He didn't love her.

Jarek cared for her deeply, and once again, couldn't name why. Loving her would be without effort. And probably not too far off.

That didn't scare him, it excited him.

He was enchanted with her, even in her current condition of too-pale skin and misty eyes, on the brink of tears that would kill him if she shed them.

"I want to marry you, Erron." He took a deep breath and waited for her answer.

Chapter Eight

"Y ou...you...what?" Erron broke away from his grip on her shoulders and took a step back. She couldn't have heard him right.

She stumbled and the ground met her backside with a *thud*. She winced. Her head spun. There was no way her ears hadn't deceived her. However, it was impossible Jarek had actually spoken of marriage.

"Are you all right?" he asked.

Erron gulped and nodded.

"Not exactly the reaction I'd anticipated." His expression fell, but he took a step forward and offered her a hand.

She took it, her cheeks heating again as he pulled her to her feet without effort. She'd hurt his feelings. "I'm sorry," she whispered. "You...you...surprised me." She avoided his dark eyes and kept her hands busy by brushing off her bottom.

The earth was damp, perfect for the plow, so she likely had a brown stain on the back of her dress now. Jarek's proposal swirled around in her head, and she couldn't demand *why* aloud like she wanted to. Because she wanted to say yes.

Even if she agreed to marry him at that moment, he'd never want her when he found out the truth. Her stomach flipped.

Erron bit her lip to stave off the threatening tears.

"Look at me." Jarek's voice was firm and she couldn't help but meet his gaze. The heated tenderness there made her heart pound. "I realize this is a shock. Honestly, it is to me as well. I…I…can't explain it. You're…perfect. I want you to be my wife."

The warmth searing her face intensified and he took another step toward her. Her heart shouted yes, and her head reminded her of how impossible the prospect was.

He won't want you when he finds out, a voice chided.

Jarek took her hand and she didn't pull away.

Erron ached to accept his proposal. With him, she could have a real future…love…children.

Could it really be more than a dream? His handsome face blurred and she swayed on her feet. How was she going to deny him?

Deny what she *wanted*?

She may not understand why, but she wanted it—wanted Jarek—even though that made no sense, as he'd stated. She was drawn to him, like he'd claimed to be, to her. It wasn't something she couldn't explain, either. For more reasons than just getting away from Norden.

They didn't know each other, right. Somehow, that didn't matter.

What would be worse, declining his offer or telling him the truth only to have him reject her?

Either way, she lost him. Tears cascaded.

"Why are you crying?" he whispered. Jarek brushed her tears away with gentle fingers and she wanted to lean into him, fall into him.

She shook her head, unable to speak.

"Erron!"

The boom of her father's shout made her jump.

She and Jarek looked at the large blond man at the same time, and she yanked her hand out of her tanner's and took a step away from him.

Jarek shot her a look but said nothing.

Norden strode across the field. Even at a distance, she could feel his fury. His shoulders were tight and his big body completely straight — two very bad signs.

A tremor slid down her spine and her hands shook, so Erron made tight fists and planted her arms at her sides.

Her tanner stepped in front of her, obscuring her from her father's line of sight.

She gulped and shifted back where Norden could spot her. Being blocked, protected from him, would only make him angrier.

Her father reached them in moments, glaring at the tanner. "Who're—" He stared at Jarek, then growled. "I remember you. The alley." His gaze swung from Erron and back to Jarek.

She bit back a wince. Fought to plaster on a serene, polite expression and banish her terror. She didn't want either male to see that.

"What's going on here?" Norden demanded.

Jarek cleared his throat and took a step toward

him. They were almost equal in height, but her father outweighed him in bulk and muscle. "Sir, I would like to speak to you."

"You are." His eyes narrowed.

What if…

Erron shook her head.

No.

Her father wouldn't harm him. Usually to the outside world, he actually had some manners. From the look he was giving her, when Jarek left, she was in for it.

He'd accuse her of something horrible, or just flat out beat her. She wouldn't dwell on what else he would do. Norden hadn't demanded she come to his bed in over a sevenday.

Erron dug deep for courage and took a step forward, stopping next to Jarek. If only she could've taken his hand. "Father, we should offer the tanner some hospitality. We're in the field…"

"I'm well aware of our location," Norden snapped.

Jarek said nothing, but his jaw tightened.

She winced. If he stood up for her now, she'd be the one to pay when he left. "The tanner is our guest," she pressed, her heart thundering, her stomach tight and achy.

Her father grunted. "I suppose so. Put Angus away. The sun sets soon. It's almost time for you to prepare supper, anyway." He turned on his heel without another word. Norden crossed the field and headed into the barn.

Jarek shot a look at her, and she shook her head. He took her cue and said nothing until her father was well out of earshot, but the tanner's shoulders were tight and his fists clenched at his sides, his knuckles white. He was furious, seething as much as Norden had been.

Erron said nothing, returning to the plow and unhooking one side from Angus's hitch.

The old gelding nickered and she patted his rump.

Her tanner handled the other side, his movements jerky. "I'm not leaving you here, no matter what he says."

Her heart skipped at his vow, and she bit her bottom lip. "This is my life, Jarek."

"And there's something very wrong with it."

She shook her head. Blinked to clear her vision when new tears arose; Erron fought the urge to sniffle. He couldn't see her face from her current position, and it was for the better.

"I don't like how he talks to you. And I remember how he snatched your arm the day we met. He hurt you."

You have no idea.

She had to keep it that way.

Sliding her hand into Angus's bridle, Erron tugged the elderly gelding toward the barn. "Get your horse and come this way, but please keep your thoughts in your head. My father is in the barn. Leave the plow, I'll get it later."

Jarek growled and grabbed her arm. Although his

touch was urgent, he didn't hurt her. "I promised you in Dalunas Main I was coming for you, and I have. I'm telling you now. I'm not leaving you here, Erron."

She stared at him, tears hot on her cheeks. "You won't want me, Jarek."

Why did I say that?

"What are you talking about? I *do* want you. I want you to be my wife."

Shaking her head again, she sucked back a sob. "You won't for long."

It took all Erron was made of to turn from him, square her shoulders, and lead the plow horse to his stall.

Jarek followed with his pretty bay mount, walking on Angus' other side, but his gaze burned her back. She could sense his heat behind her as if he was touching her. He hefted the plow too, even though she'd told him to leave it.

She wanted to collapse in his arms. Erron wanted to feel his lips on hers again and his hard body tight against her.

Even if her father agreed and gave her to him, Jarek wouldn't want her when he found out she was damaged.

Impure.

When he left, her spirit would go with him.

Chapter Nine

er hands shook as she ladled stew into a bowl. Erron's heart was at a constant pound, her skin flushed. She felt the sweat on her brow, but didn't want her father to see her nerves, so she left it alone, praying her whole face didn't have the sheen she suspected it did.

The two men at the small table were silent, but disaster was imminent.

She made it to them without tripping and set Jarek's dinner down in front of him.

He smiled and offered thanks.

Erron averted her gaze.

Norden watched, eyes narrowed. He said nothing, but tremors chased each other down her spine.

Her palms were as clammy as the rest of her, and she resisted the urge to wipe them dry on her dress. Hurrying back to the kitchen area of their cottage, she retrieved the bread she'd baked that morning. Her father always demanded warm a warm loaf with his meal, so she'd heated it by proximity to the fireplace.

She had to get her own bowl, too. Erron took her seat after pouring mead for her father.

Jarek stopped her and poured his own, as well as some for her, earning a glare from Norden.

She held her breath, staring at the inviting bowl of rabbit stew. Steam wafted, the pleasant scent tickling her nose, but it only made her stomach clench tighter.

As was typical for her father, conversation was scarce as he shoved food into his mouth.

Her tanner shifted on the seat next to her but Erron screamed at herself not to look at him. If Norden assumed they had some familiarity, she'd pay for it later.

She bit back a gulp and shoved a spoonful of the thick stew into her mouth.

Chew. Swallow. Repeat.

Normally, this was one of her favorite meals; tonight she tasted nothing.

"This tastes very good, Erron, thank you," Jarek said.

Meeting his eyes for only a moment, she gave a small smile. "Thank you," she whispered.

Her father looked up. Said nothing, but snatched another piece of bread and tore off a bite.

Erron took a breath and made herself eat. The sooner they finished, the sooner Jarek would…well, what *did* he plan to do?

He'd said he wanted to speak to her father about her hand in marriage. Would he just come out and say it?

Her heart stuttered. How could she make her father think she didn't care either way? If he figured she desired to marry Jarek, he'd surely decline.

Probably will, anyway.

She'd never had a suitor before. What would Norden say?

Erron spared Jarek a glance. Heat crept up her neck as she caught his dark eyes. He was staring in her direction. She looked down, swirling her spoon in her bowl, swallowing a few times.

What would the tanner say if her father said no?

I promised you in Dalunas Main I was coming for you, and I have. I'm telling you now. I'm not leaving you here, Erron. Memory conjured his words as if he leaned over and whispered them in her ear.

He wouldn't leave her.

He wouldn't…leave her?

Her stomach roiled as panic settled over her. Would he leave her? Why did she *care*?

This was her life, she was resigned to it. As she always had been…

He won't want you when he finds out the truth.

Erron closed her eyes, then forced another breath and sat taller. She was at the supper table. Her father was right next to her. She couldn't give Norden cause to notice something wasn't right with her.

The hope Jarek had instilled in her made her chest ache.

Whether she stayed with her father or went with her tanner, she'd never be the same.

----✕----

Evening meal was an awkward affair.

Jarek had no idea what was going on, other than the fact he didn't like Erron with her eyes cast down, head bowed, much too silent. His gut stayed tight, his heart screaming the wrongness of the situation.

What the hell is going on?

The food itself was great...the rabbit stew even tastier than Anais'.

Erron's father said nothing, just stuffed spoonful after spoonful into his mouth, grunting from time to time. How could she eat around him for every meal?

It was unappetizing to watch him, so Jarek avoided it as much as he could.

He forced himself to eat slowly. He cut bread for Erron when he took a second helping and she thanked him quietly before gluing her eyes back to her bowl. She'd only looked at him once, and it was killing him.

In Jarek's experience, meals had always been a time to share the day with loved ones. Even before Anais had started cooking for him and his father regularly, their meals had been full of discussion.

From what he'd seen tonight, Erron's father treated her like a servant. The big man hadn't even thanked her—for anything, the full mug of mead, the bread on his trencher, and multiple bowls of stew. He ate; she bustled, leaving her food three times already to answer his demands.

Jarek clenched a fist, biting back a growl. He was a bastard. No matter what he had to do, he was taking her with him when he left.

He finished his meal, declining a second portion

when Erron quietly offered. He waited at the table in silence, his hands entwined on his lap.

Her father finished his third helping of stew and finally leaned back in his chair. The man drained his mug of mead and she refilled it without comment.

Every action made Jarek even angrier. His blood was boiling by the time the older man met his gaze.

"So, what brings you here?" he asked. "You're a tanner by trade, if I remember?"

Be. Polite.

Jarek nodded, forcing a smile. "Yes, sir. My father is a master and has taught me all he knows. Our goods are sought out all over Dalunas Main. The Duchess of Dalunas is using us exclusively. I enjoy our work and I hope to run my own shop one day."

The fair-haired man's gaze didn't waiver. He studied him, saying nothing.

Jarek reminded himself he needed to gain favor with the bastard.

He wanted to marry his daughter.

"You have not answered my question." The large man's voice boomed, and he rested a meaty fist on the table.

Erron shoved her chair back from the table and scrambled to her feet.

The move was a distraction for them both, and Jarek didn't miss the glare her father threw her way.

She lowered her head and Jarek clenched his jaw.

Damn the man.

Her hands trembled as she grabbed and stacked

the three empty bowls and the baking board that had held the loaf of bread.

It took all he was made of to not reach for her, pull her close and comfort her.

Once again, his instincts screamed that something was very wrong between her and her father. Erron was petrified.

Jarek forced his gaze back to the pale eyes that matched hers.

Norden was staring back at him, his expression expectant.

"I intend to marry your daughter."

Erron dropped the bowls, and one shattered.

Chapter Ten

Norden threw back his head and laughed.

What the hell is amusing?

Jarek was torn between punching the bastard and rushing to Erron's side to make sure she was all right.

"Marriage?" the man asked. His mirth was obvious, a smile on his wide mouth, making his beard jump. "You came here seeking *my* daughter's hand? You shouldn't have bothered." Now his tone was disparaging, and he wore a frown.

Like she was dirt. Or worse.

Jarek scowled, clenching his fists. Why hadn't he brought a weapon?

"As you can see, she's not worth much. The clumsy sort." Norden gestured to Erron, who was squatted down gathering shards of pottery from the bowl she'd broken.

Growling, Jarek leaned forward. "*Do not* speak of her that way in my presence." He caught Erron's head shooting up in his peripheral vision, eyes as wide as saucers.

Her father's brows drew together and his expression was dark, but Jarek glared right back. "The lass is mine!" he barked.

"I'm not leaving her with you," he promised, and made a fist, but kept it on his lap. He gritted his teeth and tried to suck in a calming breath, but nothing worked. Jarek wanted to hit Erron's father. Or do more damage than a mere punch could inflict.

Norden's face reddened and he pounded a hand on the table. The remaining items—some salt in a small glass bottle and a spoon—jumped.

Out of the corner of his eye, Jarek saw that Erron jumped, too. She paled and hurried her task of picking up pieces of the bowl.

He cursed under his breath.

The older man had several inches in height and about fifty pounds—weight *and* muscle—on him, but he'd do what he had to for Erron. Wasn't going home without her.

Hopefully she'd forgive him if he had to pound the bastard a few times. Blessed Spirit knew, Jarek wanted to wipe the expression off her father's face with his fists.

Then again, Erron was so scared of the man maybe she wouldn't be bothered by a little violence.

He stared her father down, both of them unmoving.

"The lass is mine," Norden repeated. "*Mine* to do with as I wish. For my farm, my food, my cottage, *my* bed, even for my disposal, if I saw fit."

Jarek froze at the same time Erron cried out.

His bed?

Did that mean…?

No.

The man was her *father.*

She resembled him too much for their tie *not* to be blood. Erron hadn't been taken in by the bastard, she was his natural daughter, there was no mistaking it.

Fury burned Jarek from the inside out. His stomach churned the pleasant meal into stone. Bile rose. He swallowed. He didn't want to pound the bastard.

He wanted to *kill* him.

Jarek heard her crying and he couldn't look at her. It would be impossible for him to see her face red and wet and *not* act on her behalf. He'd grab the nearest— anything—that could act as a weapon and kill her father.

However, him ending up in the penal territory— especially the one as notorious as Dread Valley, the work camp in Dalunas—would do Erron no good.

He needed to get her away from Norden.

----✄----

If Erron hadn't already been on the floor, she would've collapsed.

Her father had just told Jarek everything. And now he wouldn't even look at her.

He knows. He knows and now…

He doesn't want you, see the proof?

Agony constricted her chest and her breathing. She swallowed back a sob, but couldn't withhold the second. How could she feel so much loss? She didn't know Jarek.

He didn't want her now. It was obvious.

Ruined. Impure.

Erron really was destined to waste her life with her father. At his every whim, like he'd told the only man who'd ever wanted to marry her.

The only man she'd ever wanted to marry.

Shards of the broken bowl fell from her hands as her vision blurred. She deflated, falling to all fours, catching herself before she landed on her face. Her right palm smarted. She'd cut herself on the broken bowl. Her hand was likely bleeding, but she didn't care.

Her heart was bleeding, too.

She heard angry voices, but couldn't process the words. Her head spun, and she couldn't focus through the chaos in her mind.

What will I do now?

Life had rarely held meaning, but what little she'd had was now gone. She didn't want to fight anymore.

Her spirit…her soul was truly broken.

Erron looked up when Jarek shot to his feet.

Norden shouted, but her would-be-suitor moved too fast.

She gasped as her father's chair went over, with him still in it.

Jarek hit him two more quick times. Her father's head jolted with the impact, but he didn't move otherwise. The tanner shook his hand as he straightened, cursing under his breath.

She froze, a gasp falling from her lips, and she left her mouth hanging open.

What — ?

Erron blinked but the scene before her didn't dissipate.

Jarek had hit — knocked *unconscious* — her father?

Why?

He hurried over to her and thrust down his hand. "C'mon, we have to go."

"Go?"

A dark eyebrow arched. "I told you I wasn't leaving you here."

Erron could only stare.

Jarek shifted on his feet and threw a glance over his shoulder. "There's no telling how long he'll be out..."

"I...I..."

How could he still want to take her with him?

He *knew*. It was *different* now.

She swallowed, her heart thudding in her ears.

"Erron." Jarek's voice compelled her to look up. Their gazes locked. "Do you want to go with me?"

"Yes." The word rushed from her lips, but she meant it with all her heart.

He wouldn't want to make her his wife now, but Jarek could still get her away from her father. She would offer to earn her keep by helping out in his shop.

If she had to see him marry someone else, it would kill her, but she'd deal with it then.

For now, Erron would be with him. That was all that mattered.

She put her hand in his and Jarek yanked her to

her feet and into his arms. Her heart skipped a beat, but she clung to him.

"Are you all right?" he whispered against her hair.

"Yes."

Jarek leaned back and looked down into her face, a gentle smile curving his lips. "Good. Let's go."

She gathered her few belongings—two other dresses, and underclothes, her mother's silver comb and mirror.

He helped her stuff them into a hide bag.

Then Erron let him lead her to the door of the cottage she'd been born in.

Jarek tugged her outside, to his waiting horse. He smiled again as he secured the sack to his mount. His hands on her waist as he lifted her into the saddle rushed her face with heat. When he settled behind her and pulled her close, she trembled.

Her tanner pressed his knees to the bay mare's sides.

As they rode away, Erron didn't look back.

Chapter Eleven

Erron was encased in warmth, and it made her sleepy. She swayed, then caught herself. She was on the back of a horse and would topple off if she didn't sit up.

But then his arms tightened around her.

Safe. Warm.

"I've got you. Sleep if you want. We should be back in the city center in about an hour." Jarek's warm breath tickled her ear and a shiver slid down her spine.

She tried not to stiffen.

He was holding her, touching her.

It was *right* and so foreign at the same time. Her insides wobbled.

"I understand if you don't want to trust me, but I swear I won't let anything happen to you, Erron." His voice was low and even.

A *vow*. But why? He knew the truth now.

"I trust you." The words tumbled out, but they were as true as his promise. He'd gotten her away from Norden.

Jarek kissed her cheek and squeezed her in his arms. "Then sleep. I've got you."

Erron quivered, but burrowed into his chest and he held her closer, her head nestled against him. Her eyes slipped shut. This was unreal, but she'd hold onto it for as long as she could.

His steady heartbeat against her serenaded her to sleep.

"Erron." Her name, soft and right in her ear woke her with a start, but Jarek steadied her.

She jolted in her skin.

Everything rushed back. His proposal, the horrible dinner…her father on his back, unconscious.

It's real.

She was *free.*

Erron straightened and swallowed for the hundredth time that night.

"Relax, I've got you. We're almost home."

His even tone grounded her…but *home?*

Where's home for me?

"Jarek, I…" What was she supposed to say? He'd saved her from her father, stolen her away…

"Shhh, it's all right,"

"But—"

"We'll figure it out, Erron. I promise. I don't want you to worry about anything. You're safe. And you always will be."

And you always will be bounced around in her head. What did that mean?

Her heart galloped.

He doesn't want you for his wife, don't be a little fool.

Heat crept up her neck, but she trembled.

"Cold?" He squeezed her against him.

"Nay." Erron shook her head for effect.

Jarek paused and she felt his chest heave as if he'd taken a breath. "Are you afraid of me?"

"No." Her answer was vehement.

He chuckled and she found herself smiling. "Good. I don't ever want that." He was so serious, no trace of the amusement from moments before.

"I could never be afraid of you," she whispered.

He kissed the top of her head, her ear, then her cheek.

Erron turned her face so she could see some of him, any of him.

Jarek's lips came down on hers hard and fast.

She gasped.

Why was he kissing her?

Surely…

"I'm sorry, did I hurt you?"

"N-n-no…just surprised me." Her breath exited on a whoosh and she faced the front again.

The gates of Dalunas Main were coming into view. Her heart sped up, reality hitting her hard. Had Jarek not been holding her close, she would've listed to the side, probably fallen.

"He'll come after me."

"I don't care." His voice was hard. "I'll petition Lord Camden, if I have to. You're not going back."

Erron's gut quivered. Why would the Duke of Dalunas care about *her*?

"Besides, if we marry quickly, there's not a damn thing he can do to take you away from me."

Her   heart   dropped   to   her   stomach.

"Marry…quickly?"

Jarek didn't speak for a long moment, and her pulse picked up more speed with every second of silence.

"I want you to be my wife. Have I not made that clear?"

A lump rose in her throat and her vision blurred, despite her efforts to stave off tears.

How could he want me?

"Of course I want you. *Nothing* could change that."

She'd spoken aloud? Heat rushed her cheeks and she was grateful for the darkness so Jarek wouldn't be able to see.

It was clear what his emphasis on *nothing* meant, which just made her want to squirm in his arms. A new sob threatened, and Erron's hand flew to her mouth to hold it back. Her breathing was rough, her chest heaving.

Jarek greeted the guards at the city gates with a wave, as they passed through. Her tanner said nothing to her.

Tears cascaded down her cheeks and she wiped them away only to have them replaced by more. Her body shook, but he held her tight; she wasn't going to fall. He let her cry.

She needed it.

His arms around her, his chest against her shoulders, his warmth surrounding her was more comfort than words could be.

Soon they arrived at the public stables her father

always used when they were in town. The stable master's son met them at the entrance and Jarek jumped down.

Erron's back was cold without him behind her, but his large hands settled on either side of her waist and pulled her from the saddle of the bay mare. Her legs shook as her feet hit the dirt but Jarek, once again, steadied her. She sniffled and swiped at her face.

He grabbed her bag from the horse and slung it over his shoulder before giving the reins to the stable boy. "I have to settle my bill, then we can head home."

She stood where he'd put her, wringing her hands in her skirt.

When Jarek returned to her side, he cupped her face and thumbed away tears. He leaned down and took her mouth in a tender kiss that flipped her stomach. "No more tears. You're safe with me and I'm going to make you mine."

Erron didn't know what to say. It was unreal.

How could he want her?

She bit her bottom lip.

"This wasn't exactly how I'd planned things, but I don't regret getting you out of there," he admitted. In torchlight on the side of the stable, his eyes searched her face, and his brow was knitted tight.

"I don't regret it either," Erron whispered.

He flashed a smile that made her heart miss a beat. "Let's go. I know my father and Anais are anxious to meet you." Jarek slipped his arm around her shoulders and they quickly fell into step, heading into the market center.

Hope and dread warred in her mind, and she leaned into her tanner as they walked.

Her father would come.

Erron took a deep breath.

Right now, Jarek was at her side and *that* was all that mattered.

Erron was enveloped by the pleasantly plump woman that Jarek had introduced as *Anais*. She hugged her back, unsure what else to do as she was squeezed into the shorter woman's softness.

He hadn't called her *Mother*, but that had to be who the woman was. Perhaps she hadn't given birth to him, but she was definitely a motherly figure. Probably his father's second wife. Anais had the loving aura of a caregiver.

Jarek's chuckle made her look up over Anais' shoulder. "Anais, you're smothering her."

His father, whose name was Kirgan, looked amused as well, with one corner of his mouth lifted. The two men stood side by side not far from them.

The shorter woman released her with a bright smile and squeezed her hands. "I'm so glad you're here, lass. Fair like me, and so gorgeous."

Gorgeous?

That was the first time anyone had ever complimented her. Someone was *glad* for her presence? When had that ever happened before?

Warmth rushed her cheeks and she looked away.

Jarek winked when he caught her eye and her face burned even more.

"Thank you," Erron whispered.

Stepping forward, Jarek's father took her hand. "It's nice to meet you officially." He leaned in and brushed a kiss onto her cheek, his whiskers tickling.

She smiled and looked into the dark eyes that matched her — *what?* Betrothed? Aye, the man she would marry. Her heart flipped. "Thank you for having me."

"Having you, lass? You're family!" Anais exclaimed.

Erron *wanted* that.

Jarek snaked his arm around her waist and pulled her to his side, planting a kiss on her cheek.

"It's getting late," Kirgan said.

The older couple faced them, his father's arm around Anais, holding her like Jarek held Erron.

She didn't want to be parted from Jarek, but they weren't married yet.

Where would she sleep?

"Lass, I've a loft across the way, above my shop. I sleep downstairs. You're welcome to it," Anais said.

"You don't live here?" The words rushed out and she flushed, fidgeting against Jarek's side. "Sorry, that was rude of me."

"No, not at all. Kirgan and I are to wed, like you to my lad. I don't live here, *yet.*"

Jarek's father and Anais gazed at each other and

smiled. *Love.* So much love.

Erron's heart skipped and she looked up at Jarek. What did she feel for him? Something strong, surely.

How?

They hadn't known each other long enough for it to make any sense. But the *l-word* hovered in her thoughts, and she had to call herself a fool for that.

It was natural for her to be grateful—he'd taken her away from Norden, but the warmth and affection she had for Jarek were so much more than *grateful*.

It doesn't make sense.

Somehow, that knowledge failed to chase away the *rightness* of it all hovering over them as she stood at Jarek's side.

"I'll get the bed made up for you, lass," Anais said.

"I can help," Erron said.

"Nonsense. Say goodnight to my lad." The woman smiled and gestured to Jarek.

She nodded, what choice did she have? Besides, she wanted to be with her betrothed as long as she could manage.

Hand in hand, Anais and Kirgan slipped out of the living area of the tanning shop.

Erron was alone with Jarek.

Her heart thundered. "I want to stay with you," she blurted.

Jarek's smile made her stomach somersault. "I want that, too. But Anais would tan my hide." He pulled her into his arms and she sighed against him.

Safe. Warm.

Cherished?

"It'd be worth it, mind you," he said, winking and kissing her forehead when she looked up at him again.

Erron smiled.

"Let's head over there, too," he whispered after pressing a tender kiss to her mouth.

She nodded but her heart was heavy as Jarek lead to her to Anais' home and shop. He'd explained the older woman was a master weaver, but she didn't take the time to be fascinated, or contemplate learning a real trade when Jarek said Anais would train her.

Erron just didn't want to be parted from him.

Several hours later, she tossed and turned on the unfamiliar pallet. It wasn't uncomfortable, but sleep had abandoned her. The unbelievable day marched across her mind over and over. She was *away* from her father.

Free.

A handsome young tanner made her toes curl when he kissed her and wanted to *marry* her despite her past.

She grinned in the darkness.

Noise at the door of the small attic loft made her roll over on the pallet. Her stomach fluttered but she forced a breath.

No one was coming to harm her.

Jarek peeked in, a lantern held in front of his face. "Are you sleeping?" he whispered loudly.

"No." Erron pushed herself up. She sat, waiting for her betrothed.

He had to duck to slip inside the short door, but he closed it silently, his lantern casting shadows. Jarek hung it on a hook near the door, illuminating the room in a pleasantly dim glow.

"I thought Anais would tan your hide if you came to me," she said, but she wasn't bothered in the least. She was relieved to see him. Maybe he'd stay with her.

Jarek grinned pure mischief and her tummy somersaulted, her heart picking up speed as he took a seat on the end of her narrow bed. "I pretended not to hear her sneak into my father's room and waited until they were…busy."

She laughed and he inched closer. Erron reached for his hand, and he entwined their fingers.

"I'm shocked, actually. She's always so proper," Jarek said, bringing their joined hands to his mouth and pressing a kiss into her knuckles.

"Well, they're both grown." Her breathing was rushed as his dark eyes locked onto hers and he came even closer.

"So are we," he whispered just before he covered her mouth with his, tugging her to him.

She melted into him, slipping her arms around his neck. Warmth spread over her body and Erron moved her mouth under his, their tongues dancing. Heat pooled between her legs, startling her as she recognized *desire*. She wanted Jarek.

How could she even think about intimacy with a man after what she'd lived through? The thought caught her unawares, but she kept her mouth moving under his. Erron didn't know where the desire had come from, but it felt *right*. That gave her courage to go with it. Hold Jarek tighter. Show him she wanted him. She wanted to give him what her father had always taken. She shuddered, banishing the horrible memories.

Erron was with Jarek.

Norden had no place in this room.

Jarek kissed her harder, pulling her even closer, her breasts flattening against his hard chest.

She moaned into his mouth and shivered, clinging to him.

He froze, pulling back from their kiss. "Oh, Erron. Blessed Spirit, I'm so sorry. I—" He'd misinterpreted her body's tremble.

"It's all right," she said quickly, leaning up to kiss him again. It was quick and left him staring, his gaze searching her face.

Erron looked down, heat rushing her face. "I want to be with you," she whispered. "I want to marry you."

Jarek tilted her face up with gentle hands. "If you never wanted a man to touch you again, I wouldn't blame you."

"How can you want me?" The whisper fell from her lips. She swallowed against the sudden lump in her throat. She'd told herself she wouldn't ask him that question—ever. The first bout of nerves and it'd come right out. Erron frowned.

His brow furrowed. "You know what happened to you isn't your fault. Don't you?"

She didn't answer—couldn't. It'd never occurred to her before, and shattered all the good feelings from his kisses.

Did she blame herself for her father's actions?

After all these turns?

"Erron." Her name was hard and she blinked. He was angry, but not *at* her. "Don't tell me you're letting that bastard saddle you with guilt. Fathers are not supposed to rape their daughters."

Erron winced. That word *hurt*. Tears welled and spilled.

"Please don't cry." Jarek thumbed away her tears, kissing her cheeks, forehead, and then pressing his lips against hers. "I'm sorry. So sorry."

She sniffled and let him pull her back against his chest, one big hand making warm circles as he rubbed her back.

"What he did to you, it was *not* your fault. I want to geld the bastard. I'm so sorry you went through that. If I could take it away, erase it, I would—" Her betrothed's voice broke, and the fact he was affected by what Norden had done to her stole her breath—her words.

Erron couldn't answer him. She let herself be enveloped by his warmth. She was safe. Her eyes drifted closed. Time passed, but was it minutes or hours?

"Erron?"

His whisper lifted her head.

Their gazes locked.

"I know it makes no sense whatsoever, but I have to tell you something."

"Hmmm?" she asked, biting back a yawn.

"I love you."

Chapter Twelve

How and why should've been instinct. As Erron met his dark eyes in the dimness of Anais' loft, her heart echoed his. Everything clicked.

It made sense — as if it was *fated.*

"I love you, too." She smiled.

Jarek stared in silence.

"I know it doesn't make any sense," they spoke at the same time, paused, then shared a laugh.

"I'm staying with you tonight."

"I wouldn't have it any other way," she whispered.

"I won't…touch you…in any way you don't wish. But I need to hold you to convince myself this is real."

Her newborn desire warred with nerves — and a touch of embarrassment. Erron's face, no, her whole body, was hot.

This man was saying these things to *her*?

About *her*?

He leaned down, slanting his mouth over hers. There was no urgency in the kiss like before. Tenderness and languorous heat made her inch closer, wrapping her arms around him.

Blessed Spirit, she really did love Jarek.

---❀---

She *loved* him, too.

Jarek's heart pounded in his ears as Erron slipped her tongue against his. Her arms tightened around him and he pulled her closer, her breasts pressing into his chest.

Thin fabric was all that separated her body from his. He was hard as a rock, his erection throbbing at the idea of her naked in his arms.

Slow. Down.

He tugged away from the kiss before he did something stupid, like push her down and whip up her chemise. Her bastard father had probably done that.

Erron gasped, her sky blue eyes going wide and starting to clear the passionate haze. "What's wrong?" she whispered.

"I want you." His voice cracked. "And that's not fair to you."

Her already rosy cheeks flushed an even deeper red, but Jarek framed her face before she could look away. "You've already been through too much. I'm sorry. I need to...*will*...be fair to you. I should go home."

"No." Her protest was almost a shout. "I want you to stay with me." This was a whisper, and her hands opened and closed on his forearms.

He swallowed and studied her, holding her cheeks gently with both hands. Tears hovered in Erron's beautiful eyes, making his heart stutter.

"I've never spoken of it," she started. She sucked in air, but maintained his gaze.

More tears would kill him, but Jarek would let her talk if she needed to. "Do you want to?" he whispered.

"I don't know." Her bottom lip wobbled.

"Whatever you need, I'm here for you. No matter what." He drew her back into his arms. "I love you," he whispered into her downy hair. Her long white-blonde locks were finally loose, flowing down her back and he smoothed his hand over them. Softness teased and wrapped around his fingertips. Touching her felt good…*right*.

When was the last time that bastard had raped her?

It was better for him not to know.

Blessed Spirit, I want to gut him.

"Jarek?"

His name was muffled against his shirt.

"Hmmm?"

She lifted her head and their eyes locked. "I need you to know something."

"What, love?"

Erron paused at the endearment.

He pressed a kiss into her forehead.

"I…I…" When she faltered, he squeezed her hand to give her strength. Her breasts rose and fell as she took a deep breath. "I've been with a man, and I never wanted that. But I do want you. I've never felt the way you make me feel."

Jarek stared.

What could he say?

She was the strongest person he'd ever met.

He kissed her, intending something slow and tender that quickly became more. Erron pressed ever closer, their tongues dueling. Her hands were all over him, and that didn't help his self-control.

Panting, he pulled away before he wouldn't be able to, but she clung to him, squeezing her arms around him.

The first hot tears hit his neck and he just held her, rubbing her back. Her crying was killing him, but she needed to get it all out.

Then, like he'd told her, he'd listen if she needed to talk. *When* she needed to talk. It would all have to come out eventually.

Jarek would have to restrain himself from going after the bastard and gelding him.

Whispering into her hair that he loved her, he held her close until Erron's sniffles finally lessened. When she looked up at him, he wiped her tears away.

"I love you, too."

He dropped a kiss on her nose. "Good."

"Want to get into bed with me?" Erron asked. Her cheeks flushed pink, but she met his gaze head on. "I don't know…what…I'm ready for."

His heart flipped. "Shhh. Don't worry about anything. I'll be here for you when you're ready. It happens on *your* terms, Erron."

She offered a tremulous smile. "I love when you hold me."

Jarek smiled back. "Good thing I love holding you, then."

Erron laughed and it was the best sound he'd ever heard.

He crawled into the small bed next to her, yanked the sleeping furs up and gathered her to him. Closing his eyes, he let the love…the rightness…wash over him. He could hold Erron forever. And he'd get to. She was going to be his wife.

"Jarek?" she whispered as she snuggled closer, resting her head on chest.

"Yes, love?"

"My father will come for me."

Pressing a kiss into the crown of her head, he sighed. "I know."

"What are we going to do?"

"We'll deal with it in the morning. But I promise I won't let him take you away from me."

Chapter Thirteen

ounding. Yelling.

What's going on?

Jarek sat up and rubbed his eyes. With a wide yawn, he oriented himself.

Ah, that's right.

Anais' loft.

Erron.

He looked down at the women nestled against him. The woman he would marry. The woman he loved. Jarek smiled and leaned down, pushing a soft kiss on her mouth as she slept.

Erron stirred and smiled, her breasts heaving with a breath. Her gorgeous summer-sky eyes fluttered as she came around, tender smile still curving her full mouth.

"Morning," he whispered.

"Morning," she echoed, slipping her arm around his waist and squeezing.

He caressed her cheek and brushed her flaxen locks from her face.

The noise outside increased, and Jarek glanced toward the small loft window when he heard a familiar voice shouting.

Da.

He frowned and glanced at Erron.

Her eyes went wide, no trace of sleepiness remaining. She shoved to a sitting position and yanked the white linens to her chin. Her skin was as void of color as they were. "My father." The two words shook.

"My father, as well." Jarek pressed a quick kiss to her lips, but she didn't react. "Stay there." He slipped from the small pallet and slunk to the window.

Kirgan was shirtless, breeches held up with a hand, glaring at Norden.

The taller man had an axe in hand.

Anais hovered in the doorway of the shop, long blonde hair loose and mussed. She clutched a cloak around her body.

"Son of a—" He cut off his curse at Erron's whimper. No use worrying her more than she already was. Jarek winced.

Would her father use the tool as a weapon? Was his da's life in danger?

The gasp at his elbow made him glance down.

"You should've stayed in bed, love," he admonished. There was no reason for her to witness the scene below.

Her hand was over her mouth, her eyes filled with tears. "He wouldn't..." She paled even more than moments before.

He put both hands on her shoulders and squeezed gently. "Shhh. I'm going down there. But you have to *promise* you'll stay here."

Erron swallowed, but nodded, her blue eyes misty

and wide.

"It'll be all right, love," he said. "I won't let him hurt us or take you away."

Jarek kissed her hard and fast, then stomped into his boots. He raced down from the loft and out Anais' front door.

Catching his father's gaze first, Kirgan's eyes widened, but he said nothing.

Erron's father glared as Jarek slid between Norden and his father. The surprise must've knocked him off balance, because he dropped the axe.

It clattered to the ground and Kirgan grabbed it.

"Give me my daughter," the man barked.

A wave of satisfaction rolled over him at the sight of Norden's bruised face. The man hadn't even bathed. Dried blood threaded throughout his beard under his nose. It was a wonder he could see out of two swollen eyes.

"You can return home. Erron stays with me."

The large man growled and launched forward. He snatched Jarek by the tunic with both fists.

Kirgan uttered a protest and Anais yelled his name.

"Unhand my son," his father commanded.

"Give me my daughter," Norden repeated, spittle leaking from the corners of his mouth.

Jarek winced as foul breath hit his face. His stomach roiled, but he made no move to pull away from the taller, bulkier man. "I *will not* let you rape her again," he bit out.

Anais gasped.

Norden's fair eyebrows drew even tighter, but he didn't deny the statement right away. "The lass has filled your ears with tales." His eyes—a match for Erron's—darted over Jarek's shoulder, from his father to Anais. The apple of his throat jumped a few times.

So he didn't want anyone to know what he'd confessed.

Jarek threw his head back and laughed.

Norden roared, but released him.

He stepped closer, growling. "You know damn well *she* told me nothing. You're a monster. Harming your child in the worst way possible. You should've been protecting her, been her *father*."

Erron's father said nothing, but his jaw clenched and he flexed his giant fists.

"I'm going to petition Lord Camden this morning and file charges against you. Explain *exactly* what went on between you and your *daughter*."

Stumbling back, Norden's eyes went wide and he paled, as badly as Erron had up in the loft.

Jarek scowled. *Coward bastard.* Fear looked good on him.

"Lies. All lies," the big man muttered, shaking his head. His shoulders slumped, his bravado gone.

Kirgan stepped forward and thrust out Norden's axe. "Even if she wasn't to marry my son, *I'd* never allow Erron to go back with you."

Jarek's chest swelled. His father's support without question gave him strength. "Expect Lord Camden's proclamation soon," he told his betrothed's father.

Norden shook his head again, sputtering nonsensical words.

"If he doesn't commit you to the penal territory, I'd be shocked. And if you come after us, or lay even a finger on Erron again, I will kill you."

---✖---

"I don't want you to go to Lord Camden," Erron blurted as she rushed into the tanning shop.

Jarek, Kirgan, and Anais were huddled not far from each other just inside the doorway.

As she'd stared out of the window of the loft, her heart thudded with every step of her father's retreat. She'd heard every word they'd exchanged.

He'd *hurried* away.

Norden hadn't even looked back.

What could he be planning?

Was he gone, out of her life, for good?

It couldn't be that simple. He'd told her many times he'd never let her go.

Jarek rushed over and tugged her into his arms. "Love—"

Erron squeezed him tightly before pulling back. "I just…want to be with you. I…*need* to be done with him. I can't…don't want to have to tell…" Her voice broke on a sob. There was no way she could testify to the Duke of Dalunas about what her father had done to her.

"Shhh…" Her betrothed squeezed her against him, rocking her gently.

Anais stroked her back as her tanner held her.

She tried to catch her breath. She shut her eyes and wiped away her tears.

Why didn't she *want* revenge on the man who should've never taken her innocence? A man whose blood flowed through her veins?

Erron should *want* him to rot in Dread Valley, but she only wanted to be away from her father.

To be with Jarek.

And…now she had both?

"He needs to pay for what he did to you," Jarek said into her hair.

"The lass should have the say," Anais answered. Her small hand continued to make soothing circles up and down Erron's back.

She didn't even know the older woman, but felt cherished already, and that she'd gained not one champion, but three.

Family.

Jarek released her and the four of them moved to the living quarters of the two men, separate from the shopfront. Her betrothed seated her at the table while his father and mother-to-be disappeared into Kirgan's sleeping room. They emerged moments later, fully dressed and groomed; Anais had gathered her long blonde locks into a bun.

Taking a seat across from Erron, Jarek's father reached for her hand. His deep brown eyes were impossibly soft, concerned. "What that man did to you is wrong. You have a right to see him punished. The duke is a good man. He would hold a trial."

She shook her head. Panic clawed at her and she panted.

Jarek scooted his chair closer, throwing his arm around her shoulders and pulling her against his side.

"I just want away from him." She pushed words out, breathing in and out slowly, deliberately. Her tanner's touch helped ground her.

The men exchanged a look but said nothing.

Anais put a plate of fresh bread and a bowl of butter on the table next to some fruit that had already been there. She rested her hand on Erron's shoulder. "You two eat, and leave the lass alone. She's made it clear how it'll be handled."

Jarek and Kirgan protested, but Erron met the older woman's eyes, giving a grateful smile.

The older woman caressed her cheek and smiled back. "You're here now, lass. You're safe, and soon to belong to my lad. He'll treat you right. Love you and care for you."

She nodded. She believed Anais. She'd finally be a part of a real family.

Kirgan and the woman would be like parents to her. Erron could have a mother again. Then she could *be* a mother. She and Jarek would have children.

"Erron, I don't think—"

"Hush, you." Anais admonished, cutting off Jarek's statement.

Her tanner's brow drew tight, but he said nothing.

"There are many types of justice," she added

softly.

"Including gelding," Jarek bit back.

"Hear, hear to that," Kirgan said.

"I won't let him touch you again," her betrothed growled, ignoring the glare his mother-to-be threw his way for ignoring her.

"That's enough for me," Erron said, her voice getting stronger with each word.

Jarek crossed his arms over his broad chest, his expression dark. "I don't like it."

"Neither do I," his father echoed.

She was cold without his arm around her but she met his eyes straight on. "All I want is you."

His face softened and he caressed her cheek. "All I want is you, too."

Her heart tripped at the sincerity of his tone, and the love in his expression. Jarek was all for her.

Norden's angry face popped into her thoughts and she suppressed a shiver. "He'll come back for me." Her father was the only threat to her happiness.

Jarek's words on the ride into Dalunas Main teased her memory. He'd said they'd marry quickly.

"Let him come," Kirgan said, making a fist.

"It won't matter," her betrothed said at the same time, cupping her face. The intensity of his stare made her cheeks warm all over again. "Erron, will you marry me? Today?"

"Yes," she whispered, elation washing over her. She grinned.

Kirgan grabbed Anais' hand, kissing her knuckles

before tugging her to his side, arm slung low around her waist.

She beamed, her round cheeks pink.

Jarek glanced at the older couple, then back at Erron. "Shall we have a wedding today? Or two?" He winked and his father grinned when Anais giggled.

Erron's stomach flipped. She would be married this very day.

But when would her father reappear?

Chapter Fourteen

1t wasn't difficult to find a priest and an available chapel.

Erron shifted from foot to foot, smoothing the shimmery ivory gown Anais had insisted on buying her. The move was unnecessary as the dress was gorgeous and flawless, but she had to keep her hands busy to stave off nerves.

Her wedding attire had a lower bodice than she was used to or comfortable with, displaying cleavage, but all three of her new family-to-be, even Jarek's father, had exclaimed how beautiful she was. She'd be three shades of red for the rest of the day, if not the rest of the sevenday.

The gown had a simple elegance that made her feel completely out of place, but it was lovely, she couldn't deny that.

Her mother-by-marriage-to-be had selected it and dressed her like a doll, including fashioning her long hair. Her locks were intricately braided with flowers woven in. Erron had never been outfitted or groomed so exquisitely. For her wedding day, no less!

A day she'd long since given up on even imagining.

Her stomach fluttered, and nerves settled over her,

a mixture of excitement and dread—the fear wasn't for her upcoming vows. She *wanted* to bind herself to Jarek.

She couldn't help but glance over her shoulder. The chapel was dim and empty save them, but was her father around the corner?

Would he burst through the dark wooden doors at any moment?

Erron imagined him shattering the pretty stained glass windows or breaking the pews with the axe he'd carried that morning. She tried to shake the image from her head, but Norden was the only one who could destroy her happiness.

Jarek grabbed her hand and slid his fingers in hers, squeezing gently and smiling.

She'd always thought him handsome, but dressed as fancy as she for their wedding; he had her heart skipping a beat. Fine dark brown leather breeches and a matching doublet brought out the color of his eyes and the long sleeved tunic was the same hue as her dress.

Bright green leaves on a vine were embroidered along the edges and around the neckline, and it was somehow fitting for him. The color popped from the dark brown, as much as it fit.

Her tanner would soon belong to her.

Kirgan and Anais would also exchange vows this day. The older woman was glowing in a pale blue gown, her long hair loose and down her back in soft waves. The style made her look turns younger. Her dress was also embroidered, but with shiny silver roses, making her appear ethereal as light caught the threading.

Jarek's father was outfitted to compliment his bride, in a dark blue kit that had silver threading trim. He looked like the older version of his son, and they were striking standing side by side.

Erron had made the mistake of worrying aloud about the coin all the garments had cost. She was hushed by more than one party, but when Anais had told her she'd *deserved* a pretty gown for her wedding, she'd cried. She couldn't help it.

Everything was surreal.

On the short walk to the chapel, Jarek had teased his father for not being able to keep his eyes off his bride, but Erron's betrothed wouldn't quit staring at *her* either. Her blush would become permanent if he kept it up.

As her soon-to-be-father-by-marriage spoke to the priest, she fidgeted against Jarek.

"Love?" he whispered. "Are you all right?"

"Yes," she breathed, smiling and forcing a nod. She was still equal parts overjoyed and paranoid that her father would appear and ruin things. She couldn't tell him that, though. The words wouldn't form.

Jarek smiled back and leaned down. "I'd kiss you right now if I could," he said into her ear. "You're the most beautiful woman I've ever seen."

She looked into his dark eyes. The tenderness and heat there made her stomach flip.

What would tonight bring?

The night she'd spent in his arms in Anais' loft had been more than pleasant, but innocent.

Would her new husband accept if she wasn't ready to make love? Jarek had told her he'd wait for her. But was she ready? If not, when would she be?

Erron had the urge to gulp.

"You haven't changed your mind, have you?" His eyebrows were drawn tight, as if he could hear her thoughts. "You still want to marry me?"

"Of course." She made herself be honest; he deserved that. "I…was…contemplating tonight."

"Nothing will be rushed into, love."

She grinned. "Except our marriage."

Jarek laughed, nodding. "Aye, there is that." His expression sobered and he cupped her face. "But it's *right*."

Erron nodded. It *was* perfect, despite circumstances and worries about her father.

The priest cleared his throat. "Are you ready?"

Collectively they nodded.

Jarek took her hand and they stepped up to the dais next to Kirgan and Anais in front of the portly older balding priest of the Blessed Spirit.

They would exchange vows at the same time, and act as witnesses for each other. The parchment scrolls declaring their marriages only needed signatures when they were done. The priest would then deliver them to Castle Malloch to file with the duke's steward in charge of registering vital statistics.

It would be *official*.

Erron and Jarek would be legally married and there wasn't a thing Norden could do about it.

Tingles raced up and down her body, but she forced herself to calm and stand still next to her betrothed, ready for the priest to give the blessing.

The ceremony was short; she spoke when it was necessary, repeating the priest's words when prompted. Jarek's eyes were only for her, and she couldn't help but stare up at him as he pledged his heart, his life, to her.

"I pronounce you men and wives." The priest winked. "You may salute your brides," he added, a grin on his bearded face.

Is this a dream?

She was married? Wed to a man she'd fallen in love with?

Please let it be true.

She didn't want to wake up devastated if it wasn't real.

Erron's vision blurred for the hundredth time that day, but this time it was happy tears. Her heart leapt for joy when her *husband* pulled her into his arms.

She was vaguely aware that Kirgan had also drawn Anais to him, but then Jarek claimed her mouth and she was lost to him.

He pushed against her lips and she didn't hesitate to open for him, her arms shooting around his neck as she pressed closer. She rubbed her tongue against his, her breasts lifting against his chest as warmth spread over her, settling low in her belly.

When he deepened the kiss, everything but Jarek fell away, and Erron just *felt,* giving herself over to him and the desire burning up her form.

She ached, and she wanted — *needed* so much more.

He pulled away much too quickly, and she struggled for breath and coherent thought, never wanting to leave the circle of his arms.

Jarek stared down at her, his gaze intense, and his breathing as uneven as hers.

A chuckle broke their spell, and Erron forced her eyes away from her new husband's heavy-lidded ones.

Where they were located came rushing back, and embarrassment flushed her limbs, cooling her ardor, but the heat of his chest against her breasts, his hips against hers was a pleasant contradiction. She could feel her new husband's erection against her, too, so Jarek had been just as swept away as she.

He made no move to release her, which helped ground her even more. Jarek didn't seem ashamed. That helped, too.

"Young people," the priest said, but the smile on his face was bright.

Erron jumped, and she wanted to bury her face against Jarek's neck. Maybe she was too mortified, after all.

"Save that for later, my lad." Anais wore an infectious grin.

Jarek and his father laughed, and Erron's face burned even hotter. Her husband pressed a kiss to her forehead before releasing her. "I love you. We're married," he whispered.

We belong to each other now.

"We're married," she echoed. "I love you, too. Husband."

"Wife." His grin was wide enough to split his face.

Erron's heart skipped its way into a canter as she reached for his hand and he kissed her knuckles before tucking her fingers in his.

Tender and protective. And so much love in his beautiful eyes, she wavered on her feet, until he steadied her, like he always would.

Could she really have a happily ever after?

Chapter Fifteen

Erron trembled as she sat on the edge of the bed in Jarek's sleeping quarters—*their* room. She shouldn't be scared. She wasn't…exactly.

Jarek would never hurt her. She wanted this. She wanted *him*. They were married now.

So what was the problem?

The day had been a whirlwind. First they were married, then they celebrated with neighbors. Anais had thrown together a feast, complete with music, dancing, and congratulations from people she didn't know. Worries of her father had actually been pushed to the back of her mind. She'd enjoyed herself, though her face would be permanently red from all the attention.

As evening had settled over them, the other newlyweds crossed the road to Anais' home and weaving shop, leaving Erron and Jarek in the living area of the tanning shop.

Alone with her new husband.

Erron's heart galloped and she forced a breath. She was dressed for sleeping, in one of the two chemises she'd brought from home. It wasn't fancy or sheer—definitely nothing to impress a new lover.

Will Jarek mind?

"Love?" His voice was soft. Unintimidating, nonthreatening.

Gentle. Like always.

He stood in the doorway, so handsome in his wedding attire.

Her stomach flipped and she offered a half-smile. How could she love him so much after such a short time?

Jarek came to the bedside and squatted in front of her. Taking both of her hands in his, he kissed her knuckles. "Nothing has to happen tonight that you don't want."

"But…we married today."

He slid onto the bed beside her, framing her face and stroking her cheeks with both thumbs. "And we'll be married tomorrow. And the next day…and next sevenday and the one after that, next turn…and the one after that. I need you forever."

Erron smiled and heat rushed her neck—again.

Jarek pressed his lips to hers in a tender gesture.

"I love you," she whispered.

"I would hope so, or today was a huge waste of time." He grinned and opened his arms.

She rushed into his embrace, slipping her arms around his waist. Butterflies flittered around her stomach. "Are…you ready for bed?" Erron asked, the sound muffled against his soft leather doublet.

Her new husband pulled back, still smiling. "I can be ready when you are. For anything you are."

"What if…I wanted to try…and…"

His dark eyes bored into hers as Jarek cupped her face again. "I want to make love to you," he whispered. "But if you can't, I understand. If you want to try, I'm willing. Believe me, I'm willing. I'll stop any time you tell me to."

She shivered but not from the temperature in the room. Erron pressed her lips to his in answer.

He groaned and deepened the kiss, slipping his tongue against hers.

She pressed closer, hands flat on his chest. Warmth spread across her body, settling low in her belly, and she wanted more. Wanted to touch his bare skin, feel it against hers. She tugged at the ties beneath her fingertips.

Tugging away gently, Jarek gripped her wrists, panting. "What do you want, love?"

"You."

He smiled and made quick work of the doublet, shrugging out of it and then yanking the ivory tunic off. He stood, peeled his belt open and untied his breeches.

Erron stared. Couldn't help it. His body was lean, pectoral and abdominal muscles defined, yet his shoulders were broad. He was all hers. She wanted to reach for him, but her hands remained on her lap.

He paused before shoving his breeches off his slim hips. "Are you all right?"

"Yes," she whispered. "I…want…to touch you."

"Good. I want to touch you, too." Jarek pushed the fine leather down, as well as his short pants and stepped out of them. His erection jutted to freedom.

Erron suppressed a shiver and continued to study his body. He was so different than…

No.

This was her *wedding* night, and she wasn't going to think about things in the past. They needed to stay there, never to be thought of—or feared—again. She was where she wanted to be. With a man she *wanted* to be with.

This was not against her will.

She sucked in air, opened and closed her hands. Could Erron…give in to what she wanted or was she not ready?

Was she afraid?

She wanted to touch Jarek…there. *Everywhere.* Explore him, feel him against her, and then have him inside her. Could she take that final step tonight?

Erron wasn't afraid. She felt only…desire.

She gasped.

"Erron?" Jarek's expression was tight, worried. Those brown eyes weren't filled with the haze of passion like when he'd kissed her. He looked fearful, too. "I'm going to leave these on."

Before she could protest, he tugged his short pants back up, over his hips and covering his arousal. He pulled the ties tight, as if that would fix a problem. His erection still jutted, tenting the material, but his concern made her heart trip.

He's so worried about me.

She wasn't afraid of his manhood, but didn't have the words to tell him, either. Erron cleared her throat.

"I'm fine. I…really am. Come to me, Jarek?"

His motions were slow, as if he didn't want to spook her, and he trembled when she dragged her hand down his chest, stopping at the ties on his short pants. He let her touch him, emitting some groans that warmed her even more.

Soon, her husband sat next to her on their bed. Jarek kissed her, melting her into the heat of his bare chest as he pulled her to him.

Erron kissed him back, scooting as close as she could get, arms around him, hands exploring his smooth warm skin, the muscles of his shoulders and back.

"You're killing me," he whispered, parting his mouth from hers and meeting her eyes. "Can I see you? Are you ready to undress?"

She nodded, allowing Jarek to undo the buttons at her neck. Erron lifted her arms, and he pulled the gown over her head. She looked away as she was bared to him.

She'd been naked too many times to count with a man who should've never seen her. Trembling, she banished the thoughts for the second time.

Her father *would not* ruin this for her.

Her first night with her husband would be special.

Warm hands cupped her shoulders as he took an audible breath. "Blessed Spirit, you're gorgeous. I can't believe you're mine."

Erron met his gaze, eyes blurry. Her voice was gone.

"I love you," Jarek said, pulling her against him.

She closed her eyes as her breasts flattened into his chest. The heat of his body made her burn for his hands on her, but how far was she ready to go?

He kissed her again, palming her breasts with both hands. With his thumbs teasing her nipples, a moan slipped from her lips and heat jolted downward, making the place between her legs throb. She wanted...*ached*...in a way she'd never experienced.

Jarek pushed her back, scooting them up the bed as he settled over her. The shock of the cool linens was a pleasant contradiction to the heat of his skin as she lay prone, and her husband followed, settling into the cradle of her body.

Erron froze as the shock of his weight registered in her brain. His chest pressed against her naked breasts. She could feel his erection against her pelvis, despite the linen that separated it from her tender flesh.

A *man* was on top of her.

Her teeth chattered and she fought the urge to push him away.

This is Jarek. My husband. My love. My man.

She repeated the phrases in her head over and over, but her muscles didn't loosen.

Of course Jarek noticed when she'd gone stiff and pushed himself up, breaking contact. "Erron."

Their gazes collided and she was able to breathe against him. "Jarek." She needed to say his name aloud.

The barest hint of a smile curved his mouth, but worry dominated his handsome face. "Are you still with me?"

She nodded.

"Are you sure?" His expression shouted disbelief.

"Yes."

Jarek studied her for a few more seconds. "I'm going to stop."

"No." Her protest was hard and fast and made him smile, which made her body relax even more.

"I'll go slow, then. You tell me when you need a break. We'll stop."

He waited for her to agree, which was the tiniest whisper, but she meant it. Erron wanted to experience more.

She had to remind herself with each caress, her husband was touching her, kissing her, and it was more than all right.

Soon the physical feelings, the desire, swept her away, and she let go, melting into the bed under his ministrations.

Erron jumped when Jarek pressed his hand between her legs, dragging his fingers across her sex, parting her pale curls.

He groaned and she whimpered. Where he'd touched was pulsating, demanding more.

"Do you want me to stop?" he whispered.

"No," she breathed.

"What do you want, love?"

"You inside me."

He stilled, his eyes wide and tender. "Let me just show you pleasure tonight. We can do things…without that." While he didn't say the word *no*, his determination was plain. He wouldn't take her tonight.

Was she all right with that?

Did she feel rejected?

She'd meant it when she'd said she wanted him joined with her. Uncertainty washed over her. "I…" Erron pushed herself up on her elbows, staring into his eyes. She wanted to tell him, *I want you,* but perhaps she should follow his lead. For now.

She'd frozen once in his arms already. What would happen when he pushed inside her?

"All right," she whispered.

Jarek watched her for another long moment before flashing a gentle smile. "I promise I'll show you pleasure." Her husband parted her thighs with a knee and came back to her, kissing her languorously, dragging his hands over her body.

Erron melted into him, his touch, lifting her hips and pushing against him. He was in no hurry, but she ached for whatever he was going to show her.

"I'll go slow," he breathed against her mouth before giving her another drugging kiss.

Like he had moments before, he took his kisses downward, sucked on her nipples until they were throbbing peaks, and kneading the soft flesh of her breasts.

She wiggled and moaned, throwing her head back and just letting him do what he would. He'd promised pleasure and it washed over her, making her want more.

Jarek dragged seeking fingers over her abdomen on the way to her center, but this time it didn't startle her when he parted her folds. He gave a groan at the first touch, and his eyes locked on to her face. "You're so wet."

"Is that good?" she whispered.

He chuckled. "Yes. It's good. My little innocent love."

Erron blinked. She wasn't…innocent. She couldn't tell him that, not when he was looking at her like that.

He hunkered down between her legs, pushing her thighs wider, and placing a kiss below her navel. "I'm going to taste you now."

"Taste? Wha—"

She gasped, then screamed when his mouth kissed her—down *there*. Ecstasy was instant; jolts of energy shooting all over her body when his tongue caressed her folds, then circled the bundle of nerves at the top of her sex. Erron's breath was gone; she had to pant to stop the spinning in her head.

Jarek kissed the insides of her thighs before returning to her center. He added light caresses to the magic his tongue was weaving, and he pushed one finger inside her.

She called out and jumped.

He stilled. "Are you all right? Do you want me to stop?" His voice was even, but it was still a demand.

Erron tried to form words. "No…it feels…"

"Good?"

"More."

"Aye, my wife. Just breathe. And *feel* for me. I love you." His eyes glowed with his feelings.

She relaxed into the mattress with a slight nod, but the looseness in her muscles didn't last. Her husband's mouth and hands went back to work, winding her higher and tighter, with each lick and gentle thrust of his fingers inside her.

It wasn't enough.

It's too much.

When Jarek sucked her nub into his mouth, Erron screamed. Pleasure hit with a force that made her vision go black for a moment. Her sex throbbed, and more heat rushed her pelvis.

She writhed and her hips lifted from the bed of their own accord, but the rest of her body, her torso, her limbs, even her fingers were tight. She threw her head back into his pillows, blinking so she could see again.

He stroked her stomach and legs, placing hot, wet kisses all over her belly and above her center, down to her inner thighs again, since they were quaking. Jarek reached to caress her arms and breasts, too, helping her breathe and come down from her first orgasm.

"Blessed Spirit…" she breathed.

He laughed softly when their eyes met. "I'm glad you liked that."

Erron rushed into his chest and wrapped her arms around him. "I love you."

He kissed her mouth and she tasted her essence there. It didn't bother her, only made her quake against him and need him even more. She deepened their kiss, and it melted into something long and hot, with only a shade of urgency.

Jarek broke the kiss on a short breath. "I love you, too."

She smiled and cuddled in to him as he lay them down and reached for the sleeping furs. Her gaze darted to his erection, still tenting the ivory linen of his short pants. "Jarek."

"Aye, love?" His lazy caresses on her bare back felt wonderful, and made Erron sleepy, but she tried to fight it.

"What about you?" She reached for his arousal, but he stopped her, grabbing her hand and lavishing kisses on her knuckles.

"I'm fine. Tonight was about you."

"But..."

"I need to hold you, Erron." Jarek dipped down and claimed her mouth with another potent, bone melting kiss.

Her thoughts scattered and she could do little but give herself over to him. "It's our wedding night." She pushed the words against his lips.

"Aye, just the beginning, love. Just our beginning."

Erron didn't argue. She let him gather her closer, hold her tight against his warm body. He was right. There was no rush.

Chapter Sixteen

Two sevendays of marriage, and Erron was in heaven.

During the day, Jarek went to work with his father, and she went to Anais' shop, where she was now an official apprentice of her mother-by-marriage.

She'd found her niche, and she adored learning how to weave on the large loom, as well as the smaller one. Every day she learned more, something new, and she was excited at the prospect of making baskets, but her new mother had told her to slow down.

One day at a time.

Erron had been embarrassed at being admonished, but Anais had cupped her cheeks and kissed her forehead, reminding her she had to learn to walk before she could run. However, she'd praised her for what she called *'raw talent'* and promised they would make beautiful things together.

The woman was tender and loving, even in the way she taught, and Erron thrived, even though she didn't require such a gentle hand. She wanted to show her new family, as well as her new husband, she was strong.

At the end of the first sevenday, she'd proudly displayed the small colorful rug she'd woven on the large loom.

Jarek had claimed to love it, and the piece now resided on the floor next to their bed.

She grinned, ignoring the rough edges on the oval mat, as well as the flaws where the color didn't match and the pattern wavered just a tad, because she'd *accomplished* something. Created something; made it *hers*.

Erron didn't demand to know if her husband was just being polite, either. She let his praise and love wash over her, promising him, and herself, she'd only become more skilled as she went along. She wanted to be a master weaver, like her new mother-by-marriage.

She and Anais took turns preparing meals for the four of them, and she reveled in spending the evenings with her new family; suppers full of discussion, laughter, and love.

Jarek claimed to love her rabbit stew more than his new mother's—which had been his favorite for turns—and the declaration had resulted in teasing from Kirgan that had flushed her with embarrassment and tenderness.

She'd thanked the Blessed Spirit Anais wasn't offended, too. Erron finally had parents who loved her, as well as a man who could make her heart skip with just a look.

The nights in Jarek's arm were likely to make her combust, but he still hadn't taken her; with as much pleasure has he'd shown her with his mouth and hands, he always wore his short pants while she was completely naked. Although he always rocked her body with orgasm after orgasm, she still ached for him. To be wholly his.

He'd shown her how a man liked to be touched, how to bring him to release with her hands, and then, even though he'd been reluctant at first, her mouth, but it still wasn't enough.

Erron wanted more. She wanted her husband *completely.*

She'd made the decision that morning she was going to seduce Jarek when they retired for the night. Wasn't going to let him tell her *she* wasn't ready, because she was. Had been.

She excused herself early after supper and bathed in a nice steamy bath in their room by the hearth. When she was done, Erron dried her body with a bathing sheet, drew the covers back on her marriage bed, and sat.

Waiting. Ignoring the clean and folded sleeping chemise on the trunk at the end of the bed. She wouldn't need it. She crossed one leg over the other and reclined into the soft mattress.

Erron was already aroused at the just the memory of Jarek's kiss and touch, so she was raring to go, her stomach fluttered with anticipation, her sex already damp, throbbing. She had to remind herself to relax; be patient.

He wouldn't keep her waiting too long, he never did.

The scent of sandalwood hit her first when Jarek

opened the door. He must've bathed out back, or at Anais' home—which had quickly become Kirgan and Anais', while the tanning shop's quarters had become Erron and Jarek's.

She inhaled his clean aroma. She loved how he smelled. Always had. Erron wanted to wrap herself in it, in him. Soon, she would.

Her husband closed the door and his eyes sought her. They widened when he took in her bare form. A smile played at his lips. "Erron?"

Erron pushed to her feet instead of waiting for him to come to her. "I. Want. You."

His hands settled on her shoulders. "You have me, love. Always." He pressed a kiss to her mouth that wasn't nearly enough.

She crowded his body, slipped her arms around his waist. "Don't misunderstand me, husband. I need you. I need you *inside* me."

Jarek sucked in a breath. "You're ready?"

She laughed; couldn't help it. "I've been ready, Jarek."

"I don't want to push you." Concern and desire warred in his beautiful eyes.

"It's been two sevendays. I need to belong to you."

He smiled. "You do belong to me."

"Completely."

His gaze raked her face, but then went lower, and stayed there. He licked his lips and a jolt of energy zinged straight to her core.

Erron seared for him. "Get naked, husband. Join

me in bed. Take me."

Jarek chuckled. "You're ordering me around, love?"

"Looks like I have to, to get what I want. What I need." She grinned.

He dipped down to kiss her, and it was a tender thing, but she pulled away before it could become more. She reached for the ties on his tunic and lifted the fabric at his waist, caressing his pectoral and abdominal muscles until he groaned.

"I got your message," he whispered.

Erron stepped back, nodded and sat on their bed. She watched Jarek undress as if it was a show, her eyes devouring each familiar inch of skin he exposed. When his erection was finally free, she whimpered.

Their gazes locked, and he stalked to the bed like a predator.

"You didn't like holding back, either," she whispered.

Her husband shook his head, making his shaggy sable locks dance. "Doesn't matter. I will do *anything* for you."

"Good. Take me." She lay back, opening her arms and legs for the man who'd claimed her heart.

Jarek didn't hesitate to cover her body with his.

His kisses and touches flamed her from the inside out, but this time it was different.

She'd finally get everything from him.

With him.

"I love you," he whispered between hot touches of

his mouth.

He drove her mad, until Erron was a begging writhing mess beneath him. She needed him inside her. "Now, love. Please. I need you." She gripped his biceps and squeezed.

Instead of fear at being trapped beneath his body, she was rushed with desire for his weight on her, the warmth of him, his touch…everywhere.

"I need you, too. Aye. Now," he panted.

She didn't answer, but watched Jarek guide himself to her with shaking fingers and slowly pushed inside. She sucked in a breath, expecting the normal pain, but a tremor traveled down her spine as the opposite assuaged her. Erron moaned and wiggled.

He felt…perfect inside her. They fit together.

Jarek stilled above her, his eyes intense. "Are you all right?"

"Yes." She nodded, her vision blurring again. "I'm…perfect. Finally with you. Completely."

"Why're you crying? Am I hurting you?" He didn't wait for an answer; just started to pull away.

Erron wound her arms and legs around him, holding him hard and fast. "No pain. Please stay with me. I feel good. I just…didn't know it could be like this."

He kissed her. "After all the things we've done together, and how we've made each other feel? Oh, love…"

She forced a watery smile and tilted up for another kiss, which he didn't hesitate to place on her mouth.

"This is the just the beginning, wife," he whispered.

"Show me, husband."

Jarek propelled forward and Erron moaned his name as the pleasure hit. It was different from when he'd tasted her and touched her with thrusting fingers. More intense, more feeling. Just…more.

She stayed wrapped around him, moving with him, under him, against him, as he thrust. His kisses were endless, his tongue moving in rhythm with his hips.

Ecstasy and pressure built until she screamed his name, arching against him. Her whole body tightened, her inner muscles contracting as climax washed over her in waves. It was better than the other orgasms he'd given her. Full. More extreme. Now she was completely his.

He groaned her name as he, too stiffened, suspended above her and his expression one of frozen passion. His release shot into her.

She felt the warm rush and shivered in his hold. That was perfect, too. It meant they could have a child.

Erron was boneless as he collapsed on top of her, but she held Jarek close, her heart pounding against his. She'd never felt so good in her life. "I love you," she breathed.

He lifted his head and met her eyes. "I love you, too." His chest heaved and she stretched up to his lips.

"Thank you for taking care of me. I mean now, and for the last two sevendays. Just for everything."

He slipped from her body and rolled to his back, taking her with him, pressing a kiss into her forehead. "It's my job to take care of you. I'm your husband."

She snuggled close. "I could get used to that."

"Please do."

Erron grinned and kissed him again.

Chapter Seventeen

Bustling around the weaving shop was a part of her routine quickly, and so natural Erron couldn't remember a time before she'd been Anais' apprentice, and more importantly, Jarek's wife. Nor did she want to remember.

As the days went on, she loved him more and more. Being loved *by* Jarek was something she'd never cease to be amazed by.

She was halfway through the forth sevenday of their marriage—and her new life—and she'd seen and heard nothing of her father. For the most part, Erron had even stopped looking over her shoulder.

Norden knew where she lived now, after all. If he was coming back, there was little she could do about it. The Blessed Spirit had given her a gift that redeemed what she'd been through.

Her husband growled any time her father's name was mentioned, so she didn't very often. Besides, she had no desire to talk about him. Think about him.

She chose to focus on her new life—new duties as a wife and weaver's apprentice. Erron loved spending the day with Anais as much as she loved spending the nights in Jarek's arms.

Her mother-by-marriage was also enjoying her

second marriage—as was Kirgan. The couple never stopped smiling. She grinned as she recalled Anais' bright cheeks at the breakfast table when Jarek's father had kissed her soundly.

Would she still blush when she reached Anais' age?

The bell to the weaving shop jangled, indicating someone had stepped inside. Erron was weaving a rug and minding the shop while the older woman was at market. She hadn't filled any orders just yet, but Anais promised her practice would soon be good enough to do so.

She looked up from the loom, and over her shoulder, a smile on her face and a welcome on her tongue.

"Erron."

The gruff voice was thick and her heart stopped. She turned slowly, swallowing against the sudden lump in her throat.

Her father stared back, now silent and standing just inside the shop door.

Erron said nothing and her pulse reversed, speeding up. Her breath caught.

Norden was a mess. His beard and hair were disheveled blond fluff on his head and face. His clothing looked as if it hadn't been laundered in a month. Which was probably close to the truth—she'd always washed and cared for his garments.

She faced him completely, standing from the loom and inclining her head as if he was a customer.

Erron was done with him, and she'd show him. *Tell him.*

Norden was out of her life.

He wouldn't ruin things for her now.

"Norden," she said. Never again would she greet him with the word he'd never really been to her. Respect he'd never deserved.

His gasp made her pause, but she grasped her new *normal* with both hands. She wouldn't let him dislodge her strength.

The back entrance to Anais and Kirgan's home slammed shut and the rush of booted feet made both Erron's and her father's heads snap in that direction.

Jarek rushed inside, his face red, mouth set in an angry line as he slid between her and Norden. "Get out. You are *not* welcome here!" her husband barked, crossing his arms over his broad chest.

"I've a right to see my daughter." Her father's voice broke, every word an obvious struggle. His chest heaved.

"You've no right to my *wife*." Jarek shook his head and sliced the air with a hand.

Erron took a step forward before her father could answer and placed a hand on her husband's forearm, tugging gently. "I want to speak with him."

His dark gaze flashed to her, his expression softening. "Why, love?" His body still blocked her from her father, shoulders and back tight.

Smiling up at the man who owned her heart and soul, she straightened, squaring her shoulders. "You've given me everything in such a short time." Erron kept her voice low. "I won't let him ruin it." She pushed to her toes and pressed a kiss to his cheek.

Jarek made a sound in his throat. Acquiescence or admonition, she wasn't concerned. Her husband would protect her whenever he saw fit, and it made her stomach somersault. He really was all hers, and she was all his.

Forever.

She slid forward to stand beside her husband, facing her father.

Jarek grabbed her hand and Erron entwined their fingers, his touch giving her even more strength.

She cleared her throat.

Was she really going to do this?

Yes.

"What you did to me, a young girl should *never* have to endure."

Something flickered across the pale eyes that matched hers, but her father said nothing.

Erron took a breath. "I'll never forget, but I'm at peace now. You'll never touch me again. So go from here and *never* come back. I've put you in my past, and that's where you'll stay." She should scream, fuss, pound his chest with both fists, but with every word she felt lighter, the sharp pain of what Norden had taken from her fading to an ache, even more than it had over the last four sevendays.

It wouldn't dissipate right now, but with time, perhaps she'd completely heal. Her husband and her new parents had already helped so much.

Jarek squeezed her hand and she forced her breathing to regulate.

"I'm done with you," Erron said.

Norden's mouth hardened and he took a step forward, intentionally towering over her like he had all those turns. He raised his hand as if to slap her, which made her husband shoot forward.

She raised her palm to stop Jarek and stared her father down like she'd *never* had the courage to do. "I'm. Done. With. You," she repeated. Her voice rose with each word.

His shoulders slumped at the second use of the phrase he'd so often used to release her from his bed. His eyes never left hers, but after silent seconds, his arm withered to his side and his massive chest heaved as if he'd taken a breath. Norden's face fell, too.

Erron said nothing, felt nothing, as she observed his defeated figure. Not even pity or sorrow. It was as if she was gazing at a stranger.

He studied her, his gaze raking her whole form, but still said nothing.

What was he thinking? Had he expected her to leave with him?

Why had the man even come?

Slipping his arm around her waist, Jarek pulled her flush to his side. "Well, go on. You heard what my wife said. She's *done* with you."

Her father's eyes narrowed and he opened his mouth as if he would speak, but her husband growled.

"You. Are. Not. Welcome. Here," Jarek bit out.

With that, the man who'd tormented her for ten turns slipped from the shop without another word.

The sense of finality settled over her and Erron's stomach fluttered.

He was gone.

For *good*.

Jarek tugged her to him and covered her mouth with his before she could take a breath.

She slipped her arms around his neck and melted into him—like she would for the rest of her life.

"Are you all right?" he whispered, but it was really a soft demand.

Erron smiled up at him. "More than all right. I'm perfect."

"Aye, you are, love. I'm so proud of you."

Her heart skipped. "I'm proud of me, too."

"I love you," Jarek said before pressing another kiss into her lips.

"I love you, too." She snuggled into his chest and her husband rested his cheek against her hair. "Do you think he's gone for good?" Erron asked after several moments of a companionable silence.

"I'm not sure, but we have the rest of our lives to find out. But I'll keep you safe."

She lifted her head and met his dark eyes. "I'll hold you to that."

Jarek grinned. "You'd better." He leaned down and claimed her mouth again.

Erron clung to him and kissed him back.

Want more Erron and Jarek? Keep READING!

Normally, I tend to write epilogues for my stories, and this one just didn't strike me that way. But, you can get an epilogue of sorts (2 actually) about this couple below. I really love these two.

A few years ago on my blog, I played what's called, The Author Alphabet game. It was actually before I was published, (I believe *Sword's Call — The King's Riders Book One* was in edits with the small press I was with at the time) and I used the opportunity to explore the world of The King's Riders. I wrote 26 very short stories about all sorts of characters — some I'd known, and some, like Erron and Jarek, who were new to me.

These two touching little shorts, for the letters Y and Z (I guess I did save the best for last) are where I met them, then decided to write their full story in *Fate's Call,* which was also on the blog as a serial before it was expanded and edited, as you just read or listened to it.

I also met many other characters, as well as got to

know some, like Cera, Braedon, Hadrian and Avery (all in *Sword's Call*) much better. It was a great experience that taught me a lot about this world I created, and I look forward to being reacquainted with some of them sometime!

There are many other stories there that could be told! (and some characters will definitely reappear in the series, some you already know, and some you don't unless you read all the letter shorts.)

For those of you who follow The King's Riders, (Thank you!) Avery's book is next, and it will be a fun one! Look for it in early 2018!

Y is for Yours:

Erron stared out the window of the cottage. Children shouted as they played, kicking and tossing a brown ball Jarek had made for them. He was always so kind to everyone.

He'd given her everything.

This home in Greenwald Main, love she'd never imagined would be for her. He never touched her with violent hands as her father had. He never forced himself into her; also as her father had, taking what should've belonged to Jarek.

Her husband had taken her from her past, moved them across the continent to the Province of Greenwald, with his parents' blessing when he'd achieved Master Tanner. He'd never faulted her for her stains. He'd showed her not all men were evil.

Jarek loved her, held her, kissed her, made love her to with all that he was.

But none of the children she watched playing near the market streets were theirs. The five turns she'd been married to him — the happiest turns of her life — she'd been unable to conceive.

He didn't fault her, but Erron faulted herself. She wanted nothing more than to hold a piece of Jarek in her arms. To stare into deep brown eyes like his, brush dark hair from a little forehead, see a smile that was Jarek's in miniature.

Her heart thumped as her eyes remained trained on the boys kicking the ball back and forth.

The blanket she was knitting lay forgotten on her lap, fire crackling in the fireplace of their cottage, but it was almost too warm inside. Her husband's magic kept the fire going.

It was a nice early spring afternoon, but Jarek always insisted she be warm enough.

Erron should start their evening meal sooner than later. He'd been given some fresh venison by a neighbor in exchange for tanning services. She was planning on preparing stew. It was Jarek's favorite.

The door opened just as she set the lid on the bubbling pot after a good stirring.

Almost ready.

A clean masculine scent wafted in with the early evening chill, mixing with the pleasant scent of the food. It tickled her nose.

She smiled as her husband hung his leather apron on a hook next to the door. "You bathed."

"I did," Jarek answered, throwing a grin over his shoulder. "I wanted to be clean for supper. Messy work today. You wouldn't have wanted my company."

"I always want your company."

He came to her quickly, pulling her into his arms.

She slipped hers around his neck, snuggling into his chest.

"I love you," he whispered, his warm breath on

her neck sending a shiver down her spine.

Erron met his eyes, but before she could speak, his mouth settled over hers. She kissed him back, opening for him immediately. Their tongues touched, then danced. Warmth spread over her body, settling low as desire for him pooled between her legs.

He kissed her harder, melding their bodies from hip to hip, chest to breasts. Evidence that Jarek's thoughts mirrored hers pressed into her belly.

"How long before the stew is ready?" he breathed against her mouth.

"Tubers were still a bit hard." Erron gripped him tightly so she wouldn't fall on her bottom on liquid legs.

Jarek grinned pure mischief and swung her up into his arms. She kissed him and he groaned against her lips before taking control. He devastated her from the inside out. Erron was all need for him, only him.

Shucking clothing was done in a blur, and to the floor they went, instead of neat or in order on their trunk.

Cool sleeping furs were a pleasant feel on her naked form, but did nothing to calm her racing heart, heated body. Only her husband could do that, and only after he was inside her.

He was on the bed lowering himself on top of her, then joined their bodies without breaking the seal of their mouths.

Erron cried out against his lips with his first thrust, gripping his biceps and lifting her hips to take him deeper. She needed to get closer to him.

Their lovemaking was fast and frenzied but she didn't care. Jarek moved in and out of her, touching her until her blood boiled for him.

Screaming their release at the same moment, he collapsed into her arms, and she held him tight. He brushed a blonde tendril from her heated face and flashed a smile.

"I'm sorry that didn't have much finesse," he whispered, pressing a gentle kiss to her lips. "I needed you. I hadn't seen you all day."

"I love you," Erron said.

Jarek rolled to his back, pulling her to him and chuckling. "I love you, too. So much."

She sighed, cuddling closer and resting her cheek over his heart. She could hear and feel it slowing from its frantic pace.

"Are you hungry, love?" he asked sometime later, breaking what had become a companionable silence.

She lifted her head and met his eyes. "Aye. We should eat."

They shared their meal at the small table in their cottage, speaking of nothing and everything. Erron smiled as he talked, telling her of his day, what he'd accomplished, and what was left of his project for their neighbor and friend. His eyes lit up when he spoke of creating. He loved his work, and she loved him for it.

"How was your day?" he asked as he started in on his third bowl of stew.

"Fine. It was fine."

Jarek put his spoon down, and their gazes locked. "Is something wrong?"

Erron shook her head and squeezed his forearm. "No, love. Everything is good. I'll finish my blanket tomorrow."

Her husband stared at her for a moment. "I'm sorry."

"Whatever for?"

"We moved here to start a new life."

"And we did. I do miss your father and Anais from time to time, but I love our life here, truly." She paused when his expression didn't change. "Do you not believe me?" Erron's question was urgent.

He nodded, but his eyes looked sad and he frowned. "I know you want children—"

"The fault is mine." She looked down.

"What fault?" he whispered.

"That I cannot—that *we*—" Tears cascaded down her cheeks.

Jarek pulled her from her chair onto his lap. His arms squeezed her against his chest and she buried her face in his neck.

"No." The word brooked no argument. "There is *no* fault."

She didn't know what to say, but she couldn't look him in the eye.

He held her while she cried, rubbing her back in warm circles until she calmed. Jarek cupped her face when she lifted her head, wiping tears from her cheeks with his thumbs. "I believe the Blessed Spirit will give us a child when the time is right," he whispered.

Erron tried to have faith and believe that, but it was difficult. Pain clenched her chest. She swallowed past the lump in her throat and forced a nod.

"You know something?" Jarek asked.

"What?"

"I'm yours, Erron. Always."

She smiled, her heart swelling with the love she had for this man. "And I am yours, Jarek."

He kissed her and squeezed her against him. "Are you done eating?"

"Aye."

"Good."

"Why's that?" Erron asked, one corner of her mouth lifting.

"I'm not sure my…performance…earlier was the best it could be."

"Oh." She tried to keep her tone very serious. "Then perhaps you should try again."

Jarek grinned and stood, swinging her up into his arms. He seared her mouth with a kiss by way of answer.

Erron clung to him and kissed him back.

Z is for Zethan

The little boy clutched his knee and sobbed. No one was around him, adult, another child, or otherwise.

As she got closer, Erron noticed how tattered he was. His breeches had long since lost their hem, and they were at mid-calf, several sizes too short, as if they were too small.

His tunic wasn't faring much better. It might've been off-white or tan once, but it was black with dirt and other things she had no desire to know about. His hair was shaggy, long and dark, and he was painfully thin.

Erron set her full basket of food down on the ground and squatted in front of him.

Blood ran down his slender shin but the cut wasn't bad. He shied away from her, his dark eyes wide and locked onto her food supplies from the market.

"Are you all right?" She shifted to block the view of what she'd bought. She wasn't concerned about him dashing off with anything. He was obviously a street child, and hungry. She'd make sure he was fed, but she wanted to speak with him first.

Those deep brown eyes darted to her and then away. He looked down, but not before she saw the tracks his tears marked through the dirt on his face.

"Hey," Erron whispered. Instinct told her not to touch him.

Tiny or not, he'd lash out in some way.

"He won't speak," a voice called.

She looked up.

An ample-hipped older woman swept the area in front of her dress shop. She *tsked* as she worked, frowning in Erron's direction.

"Do you know him?"

The woman neared, but the boy started to scoot away, shooting a wary glance in the shopkeeper's direction. She paused, and he stilled his retreat, Erron still between them.

Had he been the victim of her broom?

Or worse?

Erron bit back a scowl.

"He used to live 'round here."

"And now?"

"He got no people. They died."

"And the boy? Who cares for him?" But the answer was obvious. *No one.* Erron's chest constricted.

The woman perched a hand on one rounded side and glared, her broom clutched in a white-knuckled grip with the other. "Am I supposed to feed the lot of them? Street trash. The wee ones never survive."

She gasped. Even in the Province of Dalunas, where she'd moved from with her husband, there were places the homeless could go for a meal.

Did Greenwald have none?

"Isn't there any place for him? Where he can get…charity?" she whispered, more to herself than the woman.

"Aye there are a few, but not for one so small. He's not but four or five turns old. He never makes it in."

Her vision blurred, and Erron swallowed a threatening sob. The matter-of-fact tone made it hard to breathe.

Why didn't the woman help him?

She stared at the child, but he wouldn't look at her. "Do you know his name?" she asked without looking at the offending dressmaker.

"Nay. He usually runs with some older boys. But I haven't seen them of late." She *tsked* again and moved on, as if she didn't have time to continue the conversation. The woman shooed a big tabby cat from her porch and continued to tidy it, whistling to herself.

Erron bit her lip to keep from calling out an unpleasant name. "When is the last time you ate anything?" she asked the little boy.

He didn't acknowledge her.

Her heart ached. She reached into the basket and pulled out an apple. Offering it to him, she held her breath.

Waited.

Waited some more.

Finally those big brown eyes looked up at her, tears still streaming. He snatched the fruit and attacked it, taking a bite bigger than she would've thought him capable.

Her own tears cascaded. She swiped at her cheeks.

The little boy stopped chewing. "Why're you crying?"

Erron jolted. That was the last thing she would've imagined their first real conversation to start with. "No worries," she answered quickly. "Do you want to come home with me?"

Wariness darted across his gaze. Innocence should be what was staring back at her, not automatic mistrust.

Her stomach flipped. "I promise I won't hurt you. I can clean you up. Get you some new clothes and a decent meal."

And then what? was written plainly in his expression.

A good question. What *would* happen next?

Could she and Jarek keep him?

Erron's heart stuttered. They could raise him. They could have a son. If he had no one…

You're a bit much, aren't you?

The boy studied her as he continued to eat the apple. "I'll go." His whisper was so low she almost missed it.

He stared up at her as she stood and smiled, clambering to his feet after a moment. Tossing the apple core to the street, the little lad offered her his small filthy hand as if it was the most natural thing in the world.

Erron took it.

Rightness settled over her.

They walked through the market, dirty looks

being thrown their way from every direction. She ignored them, clutching him to her and continuing on, headed to her husband's tanning shop.

She heard the slap of his tools against raw hide before she saw him working at the rack. Erron smiled and looked down at the child. "This is Jarek, my husband."

Jarek looked up from his work, a smile on his handsome face. He stood, his expression becoming concerned when he took in the boy. "Love?" He wiped his hands on a linen scrap and tossed it to the workbench before coming over to them. "Who's this?"

"I don't know his—"

"I'm Zethan," the child announced, cutting her off. "I'm five turns old."

"Hello, Zethan," Jarek said, grinning and squatting in front of him. He thrust his large hand out. The tiny lad pulled away from Erron and pushed his hand into Jarek's.

Her heart hammered and the two males blurred before her. She was looking at her husband and son.

"Oh. She's crying again." Zethan cocked his head to one side.

Still holding onto Zethan, Jarek stood and reached for her hand. He leaned in to kiss her cheek.

"Sometimes, it's okay to cry, Zethan," Erron explained, clearing her throat.

"I cried when I fell."

"That's fine, too. I cry when I get hurt sometimes." Jarek winked.

Zethan's brown eyes widened. "You cry? But…you're grown."

"Sure, even grown men cry occasionally." He chuckled at the boy's incredulous expression.

Chatter continued and Erron could only stare.

Jarek and Zethan had taken to each other like a fish to water. If she tried to talk, she'd sob. So she watched. The wee one flashed a shy smile, then laughed. *Twice.*

Her husband showed him around the shop.

Zethan reached out, petting the deer hide Jarek was working on, but he let him explore without admonition. The child did so, while they both watched and Jarek came to stand by her.

He took her hand and kissed her knuckles.

"Is this all right?" she croaked.

Her husband gave a tender smile. "I told you so, my love."

"Told me what?"

"The Blessed Spirit would bring us a child when it was time."

Tears cascaded again and Jarek tugged Erron close, kissing her forehead.

"I love you," she whispered.

"Being a lass is tough, huh?" Zethan asked, his hands on his thin hips, and facing them as he stood next to the hide rack.

Jarek threw his head back and laughed.

About the Author

Bestselling, award winning author of romantic suspense and epic fantasy romance, C.A. loves to dabble in different genres. If it's a good story, she'll write it, no matter where it seems to fit!

She's a hopeless romantic and always will be. Risking it all for Happily Ever After is what she lives by!

C.A. is originally from Ohio, but got to Texas as soon as she could. She's happily married and has a bachelor's degree in Criminal Justice.

She works with kids when she's not writing.

WEBSITE: http://www.caszarek.com
BLOG: http://www.caszarekwriter.blogspot.com/
TWITTER: https://twitter.com/caszarek
FACEBOOK: http://www.facebook.com/caszarek
NEWSLETTER SIGNUP: http://blogspot.us7.list-manage.com/subscribe?u=296abc5983ebc51c1d4d0972b&id=fb22c e93be
GOODREADS:https://www.goodreads.com/author/show /5815085.C_A_Szarek
EMAIL: ca@caszarek.com